Praise for

Giovanni and the Camino of St. Francis

"James Twyman takes us on a powerful journey in *Giovanni and the Camino of St. Francis* by walking us through a story that will transform you and your life. The lessons of authentic trust, surrender, gratitude, and personal transformation will lead you to finding your own spiritual path. Take the journey within and step into a new future."

—Dr. Joe Dispenza, *New York Times* bestselling author of
You Are the Placebo: Making Your Mind Matter

"I love this book! Follow your heart into the forest and clear mountain air to find the key to remembering who you are. *Giovanni and the Camino of St. Francis* is an inspiring, uplifting story of forgiveness, healing, and new beginnings. This beautiful book by James Twyman is like the camino he takes you on: there are surprises, gems, and discoveries around every bend and with every step and on every page, a journey of inner discovery."

—Lisa Natoli, creator of the 40-Day Program for Transformation

"What a lovely, heart-warming story! I couldn't put this book down once I started reading it. It's every pilgrim's dream, namely, that somehow we will be transformed and begin to feel one's faith, and not just believe with no feeling at all. The pilgrim wants to know that God is there with God's saints and angels as the pilgrim goes his or her pilgrim way. Pilgrimage is prayer of the feet. Thank you for risking a story full of miracles and helping the reader believe that miracles do happen in our seemingly ordinary daily lives."

—Fr. Murray Bodo, OFM, bestselling author of
Francis: The Journey and the Dream

"*Giovanni and the Camino of St. Francis* is a beautiful awakening to the mysterious forces of love deeply at work in our lives; if only we overcome the stories of who we think we are, and trust the divine impulses in our hearts. When we let go of believing we know anyone or anything completely, healing happens."

—Sonia Choquette, *New York Times* bestselling author of
The Answer Is Simple: Love Yourself, Live Your Spirit!

"Life is meant to be an invigorating adventure, a revealing, revitalizing, and reinvigorating journey of many discoveries. Any pilgrim walking a camino of life and faith becomes intimately aware of the precious steps of their journey; simple daily encounters become profound spiritual realizations. James Tywman has walked this pilgrimage as a troubadour of peace. *Giovanni and the Camino of St. Francis* brings one on a camino of faith, step-by-step, into the face of the God as one seeks the intimacy of one's own soul. Anna, who has given up on God, learns from Giovanni the openness of a heart that she has long sought and found. The path that Anna and Giovanni walk is in the life and steps of the beloved herald and patron of peace, St. Francis of Assisi. Walk with these two souls in their adventurous journey, and you will find your own heart held in the wonder of discovery"

—Fr. Larry Gosselin, OFM, author of *I Have Been Waiting for You:
A Personal and Spiritual Journey with Saint Theresa of Calcutta*

"James Twyman's delightful tale of a woman's journey on the Way of St. Francis weaves poignant themes of trust, belonging, reconciliation, and identity. Simply and powerfully, he captures the transformative impact of a pure heart and reminds us of the joys of living for love."

—Gillian T. W. Ahlgren, author of
The Tenderness of God: Reclaiming Our Humanity

GIOVANNI

and the

CAMINO *of* ST. FRANCIS

GIOVANNI

and the

CAMINO *of* ST. FRANCIS

A   N O V E L

JAMES F. TWYMAN

BEYOND WORDS
Hillsboro, Oregon

BEYOND WORDS

8427 N.E. Cornell Road, Suite 500
Hillsboro, Oregon 97124-9808
503-531-8700 / 503-531-8773 fax
www.beyondword.com

Managing Editor: Lindsay S. Easterbrooks-Brown
Copyeditor: Jenefer Angell
Proofreader: Michelle Blair
Interior Design: Devon Smith
Composition: William H. Brunson Typography Services
Cover Photo: Xill Fessenden
Cover Models: Daphne Nolte and Lalo Molina

First Beyond Words paperback edition March 2019

BEYOND WORDS PUBLISHING and colophon are registered trademarks of Beyond Words
Publishing, Inc. Beyond Words is an imprint of Simon & Schuster, Inc.

For information about special discounts for bulk purchases, please contact Beyond Words Special Sales at
503-531-8700 or specialsales@beyondword.com.

Manufactured in the United States of America

10 9 8 7 6 5 4 3 2 1

Library of Congress Cataloging-in-Publication Data

Names: Twyman, James F., author.
Title: Giovanni and the Camino of St. Francis : a novel / James F. Twyman.
Description: First Beyond Words paperback edition. | Hillsboro, Oregon : Beyond Words, 2019.
Identifiers: LCCN 2018055629 (print) | LCCN 2018058466 (ebook) | ISBN 9781582707211 (eBook) |
  ISBN 9781582706979 (paperback)
Classification: LCC PS3620.W96 (ebook) | LCC PS3620.W96 G56 2019 (print) | DDC 813/.54—dc23

The corporate mission of Beyond Words Publishing, Inc.: *Inspire to Integrity*

To Emese Janiga, whose dedication to the Camino of St. Francis continues to inspire me, and to everyone who has walked this or any other camino: You know how transformational walking these ancient paths can be. Your example inspires so many.

CONTENTS

Author's Note

St. Francis has been chasing me my entire life.

At age eighteen, I entered the Order of the Conventual Franciscans, one of three main branches of the community founded by the poor man from Assisi. I was seduced by the romantic saint so often portrayed in garden statues and sentimental myths. These days St. Francis is often reduced to a nature-loving hippie, preaching to the birds or communing with wolves. But when we explore his real spirituality, St. Francis becomes a more polarizing figure—one whose intense aestheticism feels antiquated and even distasteful.

But this is not the Francis who sunk his hooks into me as a child. For me, his life illustrates what happens when someone abandons worldly reason and gives everything to Christ in order to discover the mysteries of life, love, and even God. St. Francis becomes a template for anyone seeking a true spiritual awakening—an awakening that can only be found through surrender, trust, and gratitude.

Though I left the Franciscan order after only two years, I've been haunted by him ever since. I've considered returning many times, and even acted on that impulse at least twice. But something has kept pushing me away, as if I knew I would never find what I was seeking in an institution, no matter how sincerely I looked. It would only come through silence and prayer, and that is the work to which I'm now dedicated.

I wrote most of this book from what I call the Bird's Nest, a small rooftop hermitage where I live, in Ajijic, Mexico. As I write these words, I'm looking out over Lake Chapala, a region so creatively potent that for decades it has attracted spiritual leaders, like the great Indian saint Paramahansa Yogananda, who visited the area in 1929 and called it a region of immense spiritual importance. It has also drawn writers, such as D.H. Lawrence, Tennessee Williams, Ernest Hemingway, and even musicians, such as The Grateful Dead.

As I sit here, overlooking the steeple of San Andres Catholic Church and the tiny chapel in Ajijic's main square, I am reminded that the real story of St. Francis isn't told through legends, but through an intense exploration of the modern world—its grandeur as well as its grandiosity. In this spirit, I present this story.

From this rooftop sanctuary I can hear Paul—one of our residents at Namaste Lake Chapala—playing his Native American flute, and the happy sound of my friend Joyce's three-year-old daughter Christina playing with Gracie, our community Ibizan hound. I feel blessed to have the space to reflect on the gifts St. Francis has brought to my life and to focus on the task of writing this wonderful story that has been swimming through my mind since I first walked the Camino of St. Francis in 2011.

I feel fortunate to have led groups along the Italian Camino three times—first from Assisi to Rome, then from the Sanctuary of La Verna to Assisi, and finally from Assisi to the Reiti Valley. Each time this story took root inside me, yet it has taken me many years to sit down and breathe life into the lungs of the characters of Anna and Giovanni, whom you are about to meet. They finally found their voices as I sat gazing out over Lake Chapala. I wanted to wait until I didn't have a choice, until I felt like a woman nine months pregnant, unable to delay the imminent birth. That's exactly how it felt these last few weeks, sitting in my writing chair looking over the town of Ajijic. I knew how the story began and how it ended, but the rest was still a mystery to me. I had to discover it on my own, just as you're about to.

Buon Cammino!
James Twyman

1

LA VERNA

Towering birch, fir, maple, and ash trees hung over the ancient monastery, looking like long, boney fingers reaching toward the woman as she slowly climbed the steps leading to the sanctuary entrance. La Verna, the Franciscan friary in the Tuscan Apennines mountains of central Italy, sat above her like a fortress set atop a hill.

Anna Petterino stopped to take a final draw from her cigarette before snuffing it out with her left foot. "That's the last one," she said in a low voice only the trees could hear. "At least for a while."

How many times had she tried to quit smoking in the last four decades? A dozen, or more? At fifty-six, trying seemed pointless, but something told her this time might be different. She had the suspicion everything was about to change.

One final glance at the forest and she was walking again, stepping up to the ancient wooden door that looked older than the United States—her adopted country, the one that had welcomed her young, seventeen-year-old self when she was forced to leave Italy. She hadn't seen the land of her birth since that day.

Anna was already sorry she had come.

"There's still time to turn around and leave," she thought. "Maybe take a train to Rome and spend a week pretending to be a regular tourist before flying home. No one would know the difference. I could use an American accent and adopt an air of pretentiousness, maybe even befriend a group of women from Tulsa or Atlanta and convince them it's my first visit to the Eternal City. We could laugh and flirt with the beautiful young Italian men, then promise to stay in touch after we return to our predictable suburban lives."

Of course they never would, just as Anna knew she wouldn't leave before the deed was done. She had to see this through.

La Verna was more than a typical friary, even by Italian standards. Eight hundred years earlier it had been the personal retreat of Italy's most famous saint: Francis of Assisi. It was here, in 1224, that Francis received the stigmata—the wounds of Christ in his hands, feet, and side—during a long and arduous period of meditation and prayer.

None of that mattered to Anna. She had abandoned spiritual fantasies as a teenager. The idea of spending a night in a Catholic sanctuary was distasteful, to say the least. If there had been a hotel she would have certainly taken a room but the trail began here, so here she must stay.

But only for one night.

Anna reached out and turned the handle, opened the door, and stepped in.

"*Buona giornata, benvenuta,*" the old nun said as Anna walked up to the desk.

"Hello, and thank you," Anna said, not wanting the nun to know she spoke Italian.

"Ah, English . . . welcome to La Verna. You have a reservation for the guest house?"

"Yes, for one night." Anna reached into her coat and produced her passport.

"The Camino?" the nun asked as she opened a thick book, full of hand-written names of guests. "You are here to walk the Camino of St. Francis?"

Anna's backpack was hoisted over her left shoulder. A dead giveaway. "Yes, I am," she said, not wanting to encourage the conversation.

"It is such a good thing you are doing," the nun said, setting her pen down. "Pilgrims come here nearly every day to begin the walk to Assisi. You are very brave."

"Why am I brave?" Anna asked, not wanting to sound insulted.

"Well, most pilgrims are young, and you are . . . I'm so sorry, I'm sure you'll be fine."

"I'm old. You can go ahead and say it, Sister."

"Don't even think that," the nun answered quickly. "People walk in their sixties and even seventies. They come from all over the world to walk in the footprints of the Poverello."

"Who's the Poverello?" Anna asked, beginning to lose patience.

"St. Francis, of course. He was the poorest man in the world but also the richest, because of his love."

The nun glowed with devotion as she said these words, as if speaking about a lover. But it did little to distract Anna from her foul mood. "You chose the right profession, Sister. . . ."

"I'm Sister Celeste."

"Well, Sister Celeste, Thank you for welcoming me but I'm very tired. I would love to get to my room and rest before dinner."

"Of course. In one hour you'll hear a bell. Just follow the others," she said pointing toward the door. "You'll meet your fellow pilgrims then."

Anna didn't respond. She had no intention of meeting pilgrims bent on imitating a saint who threw himself into thorn bushes whenever he became sexually aroused. That was one of the stories her mother had told her as a child, as if it were something to be proud of. If these people were crazy enough to follow an example like that, Anna didn't want to know them.

"One more thing," the nun said, "Do you have your pilgrim credentials?"

"I'm sorry . . . I'm not sure what that is."

Sister Celeste reached under the desk and produced a folded piece of paper.

"Here it is, dear," she said. "The credentials are a religious travel document. Each pilgrim carries it through the whole Camino. When you stay in a hotel or convent or monastery, ask them to stamp the inside, like this. . . ." She took out an ink pad and stamped the paper.

"There you go," she said, handing the credential to Anna. "This is the La Verna stamp. Every place you stay will have their own. By the time you reach Assisi, your credential will be filled." The nun held out a heavy metal key embossed with the number seven. "Up the stairs and around the corner. That's where you'll find your room for the night. May God bless you and *buon cammino.*"

Anna smiled and took the key, not wanting to be rude despite the sister's religious reference and her own bad mood. As she walked toward the staircase she took a final look back and saw Sister Celeste, still smiling at her.

Her room was tiny, much smaller than she expected. She laid her backpack on the single bed and began moving the contents to the drawer: three shirts, two pairs of pants, two pairs of socks, four sets of underwear, and a bra, unpacking more out of habit then necessity for a one-night stay. Toiletries were kept to a minimum, and her only shoes were the ones on her feet, well-worn from weeks of hiking. She took out the guidebook—her lifeline in the forest that would lead her from place to place like a good shepherd.

As she returned the book to her pack, she noticed a crucifix hanging above the bed.

Ann reached over, took it off the wall and put it in the second drawer. "The last thing I need is you watching me."

The sound of laughter caught her attention, and she looked out the window to the courtyard below. A small group of pilgrims were waiting for the dinner bell. Most were young, but Anna noticed at least two were older than she. That made her feel better. She wouldn't be the only grandmother walking the trail to Assisi. Immediately, her thoughts were drawn back to her daughter Kay and granddaughter Penny in Portland, who were surely worried about her.

Anna looked at her watch. Kay was probably getting Penny ready for daycare. "I'll call from the trail in the morning," she thought. By then she would be out on the path and the months of preparation would finally be over.

Months of preparation, all because a book fell off a shelf and hit her square on the head. Anna had heard stories like that before, usually from New Age fanatics convinced almost anything was a sign from God. But when it happened to her, while browsing the shelves of Powell's Books, she had to admit it had left an impression—and not just on her skull. Anna had picked the book off the floor so she could put it back, but when she glanced at the cover the title gave her pause: "*On the Road with St. Francis.*" She opened it and her eyes fell on the words "We are pilgrims, our life is a long walk or journey from earth to Heaven." The quote was attributed to Vincent Van Gogh.

She thumbed through the pages. It was a guidebook for people—*pilgrims*, as the book referred to them—walking the Camino of St. Francis, which apparently meant the trails and small roads St. Francis of Assisi walked eight hundred years ago on his way to Assisi and beyond. Less popular than El Camino, as the pilgrims call the Camino de Santiago in Spain, the Camino of St. Francis still drew hundreds of pilgrims each year from around the world, all carrying everything they need on their backs through the mountains and valleys of Tuscany and Umbria.

"Assisi?" Anna said beneath her breath. She tried to force the village where she'd lived as a child from her mind, but the mark it had left was indelible. Anna looked up, wondering why the book had fallen. Maybe someone on the other side of the shelf had pushed another book forward, dislodging this one. She noticed a man walking away from the area, thinking "That's the most logical explanation." But the possibility, or impossibility, that it happened of its own accord had taken root in her mind and she couldn't shake the thought.

Anna reached to put the book back but then stopped. Part of her wanted to run out of the store and never come back, but another part felt there was a mystery to unravel. Why had a book about Assisi and St. Francis fallen off the book shelf, possibly unaided? She needed to know.

She took the book to an empty chair along the wall and sat down. Forty minutes later she looked up and knew, for reasons she could not explain, she had to buy it.

Back at home, she examined the book more closely, still confused by the strange spell it seemed to have cast over her. She learned an Italian woman named Angela Maria Seracchioli had mapped out the camino trail in 2004, including many of the medieval towns St. Francis would have passed through on his travels through Italy, such as Sansepolcro, Città di Castello, and Gubbio. Most pilgrims began the journey at La Verna, then walked the one hundred and ten miles to Assisi where they prayed before the saint's tomb in the Basilica di San Francesco. Angela's camino guide-book had been originally published in Italian, then German, and finally in English. Since the Italian camino was less traveled than the Camino de Santiago de Compostela in Spain, it was much easier for inexperienced pilgrims to get lost. The guidebook was essential for the latest trail updates and inside information on hostels and hotels that welcomed pilgrims.

"What are you doing?" Anna asked herself out loud as she closed the book and went into the kitchen. She didn't recognize herself. Why was she so fascinated by people walking up and down hills for days on end because they thought it brought them closer to God? She was allergic to anything that sounded remotely religious or spiritual, the result of her Italian roots and the misery it had caused her.

Like most Italians, Anna had been raised a devoted Catholic and living in Assisi amplified the obsession. As a child she had wanted to be a nun and live in a cloistered convent near her home. But everything had changed when she became a teenager. Like most girls at that age she liked boys and they liked her, and when that threatened to tarnish her family's reputation, they had shipped her off to America to live with a distant aunt. Not long after she arrived, she married a nice Italian-American man and spent the next forty years pushing religion as far away as possible.

But the idea of walking to Assisi had completely captured her attention. Memories of her former town, built on the side of Mount Subasio, had faded over the years, but she still felt its influence and gravitational pull. She had firmly replaced the family she'd left behind long ago, with a beautiful daughter and granddaughter who more than filled the spaces they had left. When the man she had married and spent her life with died, Anna felt herself moving slowly toward a similar finale. Now, a decade later, the book felt like a reminder, even an opportunity. But of what, she couldn't decide. All she knew was that it wouldn't let her rest.

"Mom, are you here?"

Anna was so engrossed she hadn't heard Kay come in. She turned to greet her daughter, taking off her reading glasses and hiding the book under a magazine. "I'm sorry, honey. I didn't hear you. Is everything okay?"

"I just dropped Penny at day care. How are you?" Anna looked up at Kay's brown eyes and strong Italian features, working as she always did to not notice how much Kay resembled the family and others she remembered from Assisi. Kay would be around the age her own mother had been when Anna had been forced to immigrate to the US. Just a week earlier they had celebrated Kay's thirty-ninth birthday. Despite the challenges of a messy divorce and single motherhood, she was still so vibrant. "Was Mother like that?" she wondered to herself. "She would have been close to Kay's age now the last time I saw her." To Kay, she said only, "Thank you, sweetheart," and kissed her daughter's cheek. "I'm fine. Just been reading a bit. I was over at Powell's earlier and . . . well, it doesn't matter. Never mind."

"You went to Powell's without me?" Kay teased her. "Did you find something good?"

"Nothing, really. Just a book about Italy. It brought back memories."

Naturally, Kay knew Anna's memories of Italy usually caused her pain. "You haven't talked about Italy in years," Kay said, her face full of compassion. "What's the book?"

"Some guidebook about Assisi. That's where I lived, you know."

"Of course I know. What kind of guidebook?"

"Apparently people go on these long treks through the countryside like St. Francis. Can you imagine walking all that way just to get to Assisi? Pretty crazy."

"You've been walking away from Assisi your whole life."

The words cut like a knife across a scar that had never fully healed.

"What do you mean by that?" Anna asked, shocked.

"I'm sorry," Kay said. "But you never went back. From age seventeen until now, you've never gone back to see your family or where you were raised. And you've never taken us there. Haven't you ever wanted to introduce us to our family? Or just see how things have changed and what our family is doing?"

Anna stood up. "You don't know anything about it, so leave it alone," she said as she walked into the kitchen.

"I only know what you tell me, Mom. And I want to hear more."

"What makes you think I want your help?" Anna snapped. "I'm perfectly happy with you and Penny and the life I've created here."

Kay spotted the book peeking out from under the magazine and picked it up. "Then why did you buy a book about St. Francis? You're not religious. Something's happening, Mom."

Anna walked over and took the book from her hand. "You don't know as much as you think you do. Now stop bothering me about this."

"Here's something I do know," Kay said, "Your maiden name was Bernardone, right? Wasn't that his last name?"

"Who are you talking about?"

"You know very well who I'm talking about. I remember you telling me that you had the same last name as St. Francis and that you were from the same town. Did you ever consider that he might be a distant relative?"

"My father used to say that we were relatives, yes," Anna said, "but there's no way to know for sure. Anyway, what difference does it make?"

"You're the one that bought a book about him, Mom. There's obviously something attracting you."

"Have you ever known me to talk about God or religion? No. When I came here I left all that behind. Lucky for you I met your father and that was the end of it."

"Mom," Kay said seriously, "I love you and Penny loves you. But it makes me sad that I don't know anything about your life in Italy. I wish you felt you could tell me more about our roots. I would love it, and so would your granddaughter."

Anna walked over the garbage can and dropped the book inside. "One day Penny will be old enough to ask questions on her own, and when she does she'll find out like you did that it's not something I talk about."

That was where the conversation had ended. And it would have stayed the end if Anna hadn't picked the book out of the garbage later that day. "Kay is right about one thing," she thought, wiping it off with some paper towel. "This damn book is stirring something in me and I can't let it go."

The next day she bought a pair of hiking shoes and began breaking them in. At first she'd only walked a mile or two a day, but before long the distance had grown to as many as ten. And as her miles increased her desire to smoke decreased, though she still was not able to completely kick the habit. Now she was high in the mountains of Tuscany where she would begin the long hike to Assisi the next morning. It didn't make any sense, but she felt compelled nonetheless.

The sound of the dinner bell brought her back to her room at the Sanctuary. Anna looked around and sighed. She had come this far and may as well see it through to the end, whatever that meant.

2

GIOVANNI

Anna changed her clothes for dinner, and then folded the shirt and pants she had been wearing and placed them on top of the backpack. A small piece of paper fell out of her pants and Anna picked it up, unfolding it to read the handwritten words: *Renaldo B., Via Eremo delle Carceri #5, Assisi.* She stared at the paper for a long time before folding it and putting it into the backpack. Then she left the room.

Sister Celeste smiled as Anna walked by the front desk. Something about the nun set Anna's heart at ease, despite her long-held belief that religious vows were a poor attempt to avoid worldly responsibility. Anna remembered two or three nuns who had inspired her early desire to enter the convent. In retrospect, she realized what had seemed like a true calling was an immature yearning for meaningful connection.

Anna's father was either absent or emotionally distant, and both states fueled her mother's obsessive devotion to the church. So naturally Anna was attracted to the peaceful life of the nuns she encountered in Assisi every day.

Three years after Anna was forced to leave Italy she had received word that her mother was dying from colon cancer. For an instant, Anna considered going to her, but she chose to remain at home in the US, giving her outraged father a reason to permanently cut her from the family. But the scars were already set deep in her soul, and it was more a relief than a burden. She was an American now. A desire to return to her homeland had never surfaced again.

Until now.

"Do you need anything, dear?" Sister Celeste asked, so sweetly that Anna could only smile.

"No, Sister, but you're very kind to ask. Would you like to join me for dinner?"

"I would love to, but someone must stay at the desk and when I eat it's with the other sisters, in the refectory. I'll be with you in spirit, though."

As she'd expected, the dining room was nearly full of twenty- and thirty-something pilgrims excited to begin the journey to Assisi. She looked around, hoping to find an empty table where she could enjoy her meal alone. Not finding one, she decided to fill her plate and retreat to the solitude of her room. Then she remembered where she was—a Catholic monastery—which meant there were rules to follow, the type of rules she had rebelled against most of her life. She looked around, plotting her escape, hoping the noise would allow her a clean getaway.

That was when she first saw him.

The young man sitting alone at the corner table couldn't have been more than twenty-five, and his Mediterranean features clearly marked Italy as his homeland. He noticed Anna, motioning her to join him and pulling out the chair next to his. She would have pretended she hadn't seen the gesture but Sister Celeste had temporarily banished rudeness from her bones. She forced a smile and walked over.

"Parla Italiano?" he asked.

"Si, I mean yes, a little," she lied. "I'm American."

"An American," he said, his smile growing even brighter. "I can practice my English. My name is Giovanni. What's your name?"

Anna sat down. "I'm Anna," she said, scooting her chair to the table.

"I am happy to meet you, Anna."

Anna smiled again, not sure if she should encourage conversation. It might still be possible to get her food and politely excuse herself. She could say she was tired, which she was, and he would surely understand. But something about his manner made her feel slightly more social than usual. Why? He was at least ten years younger than Kay, probably more. But he reminded her of someone, a faint memory from her childhood, perhaps. "It won't hurt to stay for a few minutes," she thought. The tiny room where her backpack rested wasn't going anywhere.

"It's nice to meet you, Giovanni. You're Italian?"

"I am. I have lived here my entire life. I have been lucky to travel the world, though not to the US. Where do you live?"

"Portland, Oregon," she said, "for thirty-five years now. Before that I was in New York."

"New York must be an incredible city," he said, "so much energy and life."

"I wouldn't know," she said. "I lived in a tiny town further upstate called Wellsville. I never made it to New York City."

"Is this your first time in Italy?" Giovanni asked her.

Anna wondered how to answer. She didn't want people to know she was Italian. That would start conversations she didn't want to have.

"I was here when I was a child," she said, stretching the truth. "Since then, I haven't left the US."

"Welcome back to Italy," he said smiling, "and to the Camino of St. Francis. You are walking to Assisi?"

"That's the idea," Anna said. ". . . a crazy idea. . . ."

"Why so crazy?" he asked her. "Walking is the best way to see Italy, especially Tuscany and Umbria. By moving slowly you will notice things that pass by too quickly to see in a car."

"That's one way to look at it. It is a beautiful country."

"Beautiful in so many ways. It's an ancient culture, and walking in the footsteps of the Poverello will bring you back to your essence."

"I probably heard that term when I was a child . . . St. Francis as the Poverello, but it's been so long I didn't recognize it."

People called him this because he chose to be poor, like Christ. To him, poverty allowed him to live close to the earth and to those most in need. He wanted to imitate Jesus, to see God in the simplest places, like the sun and moon, and everywhere in nature."

At the mention of God, Anna felt herself shutting down and fought to stay civil, if not exactly interested. She was going to have to get used to God talk while she was on this journey. Most people walking the camino were there for spiritual reasons. Giovanni seemed kind and well intentioned, but she wasn't quite ready for religion.

"For me, it's a bit different," she said to him. "I don't mean to be rude, but I don't believe in God. I did when I was young but no more."

"Then you are walking the camino why?"

It was the first time anyone had asked her the question so directly, and it made her stop to consider. If not for spiritual reasons, why was she walking? She had been forced to leave Assisi when she was seventeen and hadn't returned, even when her mother was dying. Forcing her away had been her father's decision. Her mother's timidity had given her no say in the matter, but Anna couldn't forgive her for it. If her mother had stood up to her father, her life would have been so different. But that hadn't happened. So she closed her heart and pushed the pain away. Now it felt like a dam ready to burst.

"I can't tell you why I am walking," she finally answered. "I'm hoping I'll figure it out along the way."

"Then I will help you any way I can," Giovanni said to her.

Suddenly, Anna felt the need to be alone come back, even stronger this time. She was hungry and needed food, but she had to get away before she started crying in front of this stranger. It felt like the book had fallen off the shelf and hit her on the head again—a hardcover this time, not a paperback.

She stood, making a polite excuse about jetlag. "I understand," he said, standing to shake her hand. "I'm sure we will see each other on the trail. That is the beauty of the camino . . . you see the same people often."

"Perhaps we will," she said. "Good night, then."

"Good night, Anna. I hope you sleep well."

Anna walked toward the entrance then turned around just before she left the dining room. Giovanni was still looking at her, his smile as bright as ever.

ᛏ

"When Francesco lived here he was a very rich and spoiled teenager," Anna's mother said.

She was thirteen-years-old again, and they were walking toward the Basilica di Francesco in the lower part of Assisi. In a few years the uneasiness would eclipse the surge of love she felt for her overprotective mother in this moment. But right now she felt a magical connection and wished it would last forever.

"Kind of like me—spoiled?" Anna said.

"Very much like you, Anna, and Francesco's mother loved him more than words can say, just as I love you. He had everything and yet it wasn't enough."

"Why wasn't it enough?" Anna asked, already knowing the story and her mother's answer.

"Because God was calling him in a different direction. His mother understood but his father never did. Having fancy clothes and money in his pocket meant little, and he understood that at an early age."

"I heard he was a playboy," Anna said, trying a word she didn't really understand. She only knew that it wasn't a good thing to be.

"Where did you hear that?" her mother asked, stopping in the middle of the narrow street barely wide enough for a small car.

"I don't remember," she lied. "I think one of the nuns told me."

They started walking again, and her mother continued. "He was a playboy, which means he got into lots of trouble, doing things he shouldn't have been doing. But all the while God had a plan. Did you know, when his mother was pregnant she set up a manger in their house, including the animals, hoping that when he was born she could lay him in it, like Jesus? That's how much she wanted him to be holy.

"Francesco's father was the one who spoiled him. He wanted his son to be a rich cloth merchant like himself. He also expected his son to be a great knight, so when Assisi went to war with Perugia, his father bought him a fancy horse and a suit of armor and sent him off to battle. Most of

Assisi's knights were captured and killed, but knowing Francesco came from a noble family they held him for a year, demanding ransom. By the time he was released he was terribly ill and almost died. It took months for him to recover and when he did he was different."

"How was he different?" Anna asked.

"Nothing mattered to him anymore, especially money. But he didn't know what to do, so he wandered around and spent all his time with the poor. Then he had a great inspiration: he would become a beggar and rebuild San Damiano, the little chapel below Santa Chiara's basilica. And that's what he set out to do, begging for stones from all the rich families in Assisi. It was a great insult to his father, who forced him to leave and never allowed him to come home again."

"Why didn't Francesco just apologize and go back to where he had a bed and food waiting for him?"

"God wanted him to live only for love and to turn away from the riches of the world. Other young men soon began following his example—and women too, like Santa Chiara. Once Francesco's heart had turned in its new direction, nothing his father did could change it back."

As they reached the basilica's lower entrance, Anna's mother made a slight motion to remind her it was time to be quiet. They entered the church, touching their fingers in the holy water and making the sign of the cross. In silence, they walked to the stone staircase that took them down to a narrow chapel with two sections of pews. Anna's mother led them to the front and they knelt together, looking up at the tomb of Assisi's most famous saint, which had been hidden for hundreds of years after his death. To prevent other towns and great Italian families—including the invading Saracens—from stealing the bones to set up their own basilica, St. Francis's burial place was kept a secret until the nineteenth century. Anna and her mother had knelt in the same spot hundreds of times and today, as always, Anna felt a strong energy coming from the tomb. It was like standing next to a powerful fire and it filled her soul with light.

"Mama," Anna whispered, "I want to be like him. Do you think it's possible?"

She looked down at her daughter with the most loving eyes Anna had ever seen.

"One day you will be, my dear. God has a plan for you just like he did for Francesco."

3

The Camino Begins

The alarm on Anna's phone tore her away from the chapel, the tomb, and her mother's side. She opened her eyes, startled by her surroundings. The confusion lasted only seconds, but the empty feeling remained. Anna hadn't dreamed about her mother for many years, and she was surprised at the emotions it stirred up. This was more a memory than a dream—one that had been stored in some deep chamber of her mind, waiting for this very moment, the day when she would begin the long journey to her childhood home, to come back. Her mother would not be there. She had died decades earlier and Anna had not been with her, had not held her hand one final time. The thought crept into her mind and would not leave. *I wasn't there.*

Anna heard laughter drifting up from the courtyard again and opened the curtains to look. She saw at least ten pilgrims preparing their backpacks and filling water bottles from the corner faucet. For the next ten days they would climb hills and transverse forests on their way to a medieval village filled with friars, nuns, and tourists. Anna would be right behind them, though her path was different—a journey of emotional upheaval, not spiritual ecstasy. She wondered if she would ever be at peace with this place.

Anna heard a faint sound and looked up in time to see a small piece of paper appear under the door. She walked over and picked it up. It read *Good luck, Anna. The Poverello said that love is the key to remembering who you are. Even if you don't believe in God—believe in love. It's the same thing. Buon cammino. Giovanni.*

She was tempted to open the door, but something made her stop. It was a sweet gesture and Anna appreciated it, but she wondered if it was too late. Decades had passed since she first left Italy and her heart had been hardened by loss and regret. Walking to Assisi would not bring her mother back or soften her father's heart. Yet her resolve to complete the journey had increased, and she still had no idea why. But walking alone might help her understand her sudden need to return to Italy, and perhaps even lay a new foundation for the future. A future that focused on Kay and Penny, not the past. She couldn't go backwards, but perhaps she could heal what was to come.

She showered, repacked her clothes in the backpack, and was quickly out the door. The courtyard was quiet by the time she left, which suited her fine. This wasn't a race. Let the younger pilgrims get out ahead and give her the chance to approach Assisi at her own pace, slow and steady. It's how she lived her life and Anna didn't feel the need to change it now.

After a cup of coffee and croissant Anna was ready to leave, but before she stepped through the door she heard a quiet voice call her name.

"Anna, I want to give you something."

It was Sister Celeste. Anna turned around and smiled.

"Yes, Sister?"

"Come with me." The nun took Anna by the hand and led her behind the welcome desk and through a small wooden door.

They stepped into an office that was cluttered with books and papers. On the wall hung pictures of saints and images of Christ and Mary. At first Anna felt an uncomfortable energy rising in the center of her chest, which calmed a little when she saw that Sister Celeste was only reaching for a old discolored photo album. The nun opened it to a page in the middle and sat it down on the desk.

"Believe it or not, I had a life before I became a nun," she said. "I was called to the convent when I was thirty-five. Before that I had a career as a pharmacist, and I loved to hike through the mountains."

She pointed at a picture of a young woman with a backpack swung over her shoulder holding a knotted hiking stick in her left hand. Her smile was radiant, filled with promise and life. Though it took imagining a younger Celeste without the nun's veil, it was clearly her.

"That's you!" Anna said.

"Yes, many years ago. I loved to hike. I walked the same paths you're about to begin today. I loved St. Francis and I wanted to live my life in nature like he did. I miss being able to follow my heart into the forest, walking up and down the mountains like they were nothing. I couldn't do it today if I wanted to, but you're about to try, and for that I am grateful. So grateful, in fact, that I have something I want to give you." Sister Celeste opened a small closet door and reached to the very back, pulling out the same knotted stick she held in the photo.

"I've had this walking stick most of my life. It has been with me on many hikes through these mountains. I have no further need for it, but you do. I want you to take it on your journey. And I hope you'll pray for me as you walk, if only once or twice."

"Oh, Sister, I don't know if I can. . . ."

"You must," Celeste said, tears forming in her eyes. She wrapped Anna's fingers around the worn and knotted wood. "It means part of me will be with you, and that's the greatest gift you could give me. It will help support you as you walk, no matter how high the mountain or how low the valley."

Anna was speechless. The nun seemed to be giving her one of the most precious things she owned. "I will carry it with pride," she said, wrapping Sister Celeste in a hug. "This means more to me than you can ever imagine."

"I can imagine it," Sister Celeste said as she pulled back. She held onto Anna's arms and looked into her eyes. "No matter what happens out there, I'll be with you. Don't forget that."

Anna hugged her again, and then she turned and walked out of the room, through the monastery door, and into the clear mountain air.

Moss-covered rocks and tall evergreen and birch trees lined the path that led away from the sanctuary. Anna stepped onto the road and a short distance later saw a small rock with the sign of the Tau pointing into the forest. This was the traditional Franciscan cross and was the way St. Francis had signed his name. The last letter in the Hebrew alphabet, the Tau and its resemblance to the cross of Jesus, had great significance to the early Franciscans and now showed the path to Assisi, and Anna took her first step in that direction.

Sister Celeste's walking stick clicked happily on the rock and dirt path as she walked. Just then the sun appeared from behind a thick bank of clouds, and Anna had to shield her eyes from its bright rays. It made her smile, and for the first time since the book hit her on the head at Powell's, she was happy. Gone were the concerns about the past or what she would do when she arrived in Assisi. Gone was the weight of leaving her mother to die alone. All that mattered was that she was doing something unprecedented, something with no logical explanation. She was embarking on an adventure.

As soon as she left the road she had the sense that she had left the world behind and escaped to a simpler time, free of modern trappings. The sky was clear and the only sounds were the wind brushing against the branches of the trees and the birds celebrating in song.

When Anna had been walking for twenty minutes she saw a farmer fixing a fence along the path, his crude tools similar to those St. Francis might have used. She was starting to understand what made the camino so magical: that feeling of stepping back in time and experiencing the rich pulse of life without the hectic desires of success and accomplishment. A farmer fixing a fence—that was all she needed in this moment.

"Buon cammino," he said, tipping his hat.

"What an excellent beginning," Anna thought, smiling to herself.

She soon arrived at the crest of Monte Calvano where she could see the entire valley of Pieve Santo Stefano far below. From there she followed the cart tracks along the ridge of Passo delle Pratelle, then disappeared into the dense woods. The guidebook was always in her hands, ready to consult in case she missed a turn or suddenly found herself heading in the wrong direction.

She had several options for sleeping in Pieve Santo Stefano: a simple but elegant Bed and Breakfast a bit outside of town, the Hotel Santo Stefano, or one of three beds in the home of the St. Stefano's parish priest. The priest's rectory was out of the question (she couldn't stomach the idea of having to be so close to a representative of the Catholic church), but Anna was curious about the B and B. Thinking of the large group of pilgrims that had left La Verna this morning, she wondered how many ahead of her would arrive there. Anna felt like keeping her distance, but it was worth a try. After consulting the guidebook and asking directions from an old woman she met on the road, Anna decided to find the B and B.

It was nearly five o'clock in the evening by the time Anna arrived at the simple building. She could hear laughter as she approached—a bad sign. Judging from the noise, this was the most popular residence in town, which meant she would likely move on. Anna walked to the door and peered inside. As she suspected, there were at least fifteen people gathered in the sitting area, and she saw three open bottles of wine. "As the evening progresses, it will get even worse," she thought. Then she saw someone she recognized sitting alone in the corner reading a book: Giovanni. He didn't look up, which she thought a blessing. If he called for her to join him she might have said yes. Better to slip away while she still had the chance, so she turned around and was back on the road heading toward the town.

The hotel just outside Pieve Santo Stefano had a certain rustic elegance and the relaxed atmosphere seemed perfect. A table with a large shade umbrella rested a few feet from the front door, and the sound of classical music could be heard coming from the behind the hotel. Anna went inside and saw a man in his thirties tucking an armful of towels into a cabinet behind the desk.

"Excuse me," Anna said to the man. "Do you have a room available tonight?"

The young man turned around and smiled. "*Buona sera,*" he said. "Yes, we have one room left. The angels must be with you because we are usually booked up, but someone canceled an hour ago."

"That's wonderful," Anna said as she let the pack slide down from her shoulder. Within minutes she was in the room splashing water on her face. She took off her shoes to examine her feet. They felt raw but she found no blisters.

After freshening up, she went downstairs and found a seat in the outdoor cafe behind the hotel. An ivy-covered trellis hung over three tables, and the young man she had met inside quickly appeared.

"Can I get you a glass of wine or anything to drink?" he asked Anna.

"A glass of white wine would be amazing," she said without hesitating. "And I'm hoping there's food. I'm starving."

"You're walking from La Verna to Assisi?" he asked. "We have a special love for pilgrims here. I'll see if I can find something to fill your stomach."

The man disappeared, and less than a minute later Anna's wine had arrived. This was exactly what she hoped for: peace and quiet. The first day was behind her and Anna felt exhilarated.

"One more question," Anna said as the man was turning to leave her table. She reached into her back pocket and produced the folded document Sister Celeste had given her. "Do you have a stamp for my pilgrim credential?"

4

AN UNFORTUNATE FALL

Anna left Pieve Santo Stefano around nine o'clock in the morning after a strong coffee and two pastries. She quickly filled her water bottle and was on her way to Passo di Viamaggio, a seven-mile hike through a lush forest. She found the road that led to Sansepolcro, then turned left at the sign marked "Eremo di Cerbaiolo." The road began as paved asphalt but quickly turned into a dirt path. She was curious about the eremo, or hermitage, after reading about Chiara Barboni, the woman who discovered the ruins in the 1960s and worked to reconstruct the building. It had been nearly destroyed when the Germans retreated from Italy on August 28th, 1944, but Chiara's dedication and strong support from the government nurtured it back to its original form. The Eremo was uninhabited when St. Francis passed through the area in 1216 on his way to La Verna, but the Franciscans had established a community there in 1218, eight years before his death.

Anna was fascinated by the history. Something about Chiara Barboni stirred her imagination. She had lived alone, high above the forest, toiling day after day much as Francis had when his ministry rebuilt churches. She had chosen to take the name of St. Francis's mystical and spiritual partner: Santa Chiara, or St. Clare, who had often lived in St. Francis's shadow but who had made inestimable contribution to Franciscan charism. St. Clare was the first woman to follow Francesco's example, and her family came from even higher nobility than his own.

25

Anna remembered seeing Franco Zeffirelli's film *Brother Sun, Sister Moon* when it screened in Assisi in 1972 and Zeffirelli had attended. A movie made for its time, it presented Francis and Clare more as hippie flower children than the revolutionaries they really were. For the young Anna it was a revelation, one that resonated deeply with her desire to give herself to God. But those feelings faded, and within a few years, when she was exiled to the US, any thought she had of imitating St Francis and St. Clare was gone.

This Chiara, Chiara Barboni—the one who had rebuilt the Eremo, was a truly dedicated person. "I wish I could find something to be so passionate about," Anna thought. Her only true passion was her family—Kay and Penny. Perhaps it was because of her own history or perhaps something more, something deeper. Anna's mind drifted back to the final conversation she'd had with Kay before leaving for Italy. There were still so many things Anna couldn't explain, knowing they had yet to ripen inside herself.

"Mom, you know I support you in this, though you have to admit it's a bit out of the blue."

"Well, thank you for your support," Anna said mockingly. "I didn't know it was required."

"C'mon, stop with the drama. I'm just saying you haven't shared your past with me for thirty-nine years, no matter how many times I've asked, and now you're suddenly flying to Italy to walk some camino that will lead you to the town of your birth. You have to admit, it's not like you and I have every right to be concerned and to have questions for you. I know nothing about this place you came from—this place where my fifty-six-year-old mother is heading off to. And on top of that, I'll say it again, it's my history as well as yours."

Anna reached across the kitchen table and took Kay's hands into her own.

"It can't be your history until I deal with it first," she said. "I know it's hard to understand, and it's hard for me too. All I know is that I can't run from it anymore. Do you see that?"

"Of course I do, and I won't press you to tell me more. But I hope one day you will, maybe after this journey's over."

Anna had stood up, walked over to the counter, and poured herself a fresh cup of coffee.

"Do you want one?" she asked Kay.

"No, I'm feeling a bit jittery as it is and coffee won't help."

"I assume they have great coffee in Italy," she said. "I was too young to drink it when I left. I wanted to but my mother never let me. Can you imagine that? I was seventeen and she wouldn't let me drink coffee. That's how overprotective she was. She had no idea I was smoking and drinking wine with my girlfriends. By the way, this may even be a good time to quit that nasty habit . . . the cigarettes, not the wine" she joked.

"I never understood why you had to leave, especially if she was overprotective," Kay pressed. Then she saw the look on her mother's face and held back. "I'm sorry. It slipped out."

"It wasn't my decision, or hers," Anna said. "My father decided. It was no different than what you went through—normal teenage rebellion. But in Italy it wasn't acceptable. You did what you were told and that was it. Things happened, and my father decided I should live with my American relatives. A month later I was on a boat heading to New York."

"I can't even imagine. All alone."

"It was terrible," Anna said as she sat back down at the table. "I didn't know anyone and kept to myself for the most part. There were other girls that were being shipped away, just like me. I remember one I met named Patricia . . . a sweet girl from Florence. She seemed so depressed and hardly talked to anyone. Then one day she wasn't there, just like that. I never heard what happened."

"Oh my God, really? Do you think she jumped?"

"That's my guess. It was hard leaving our families and country and going to a place where we didn't know anyone. I have to admit it crossed my mind as well. More than once. But my Umbrian roots made me strong and I didn't give in."

"How long after you got here did you meet dad?"

"Maybe two months," Anna said. "It was arranged by my aunt and uncle. He was a lot older than me, as you know. It happened very fast. Within three months we were married."

A silence fell over the table as Kay looked down. She had asked for clarity on the subject many times, but Anna had always been reluctant to answer questions about the past and the role her father played in it. The moment had arrived for her to ask directly, and given the emotional imbalance her mother was feeling, she might be inclined to answer.

"Mom, I have to ask you something. . . ."

"No. You don't," Anna said, trying to cut her off.

"Really? Are you going to keep this from me the rest of my life? How many times have I tried to get you to tell me my own history? If there was another. . . ."

"Yes, I was pregnant," Anna exclaimed. "I'm sorry I never told you but I'm sure you did the math and figured it out all by yourself. Now you're wondering who your real father was."

"You don't have to tell me," Kay said quietly, almost afraid to hear the truth.

"No, you want to know so I'm going to tell you. The important thing to remember is the man you knew as your father was all you needed. He was your dad. What difference does it make that I was a crazy teenager and got knocked up by an Italian boy I hardly remember? It was only one night and I never saw him again. He lived in southern Italy and was in Assisi visiting his family. He didn't even tell me he was leaving and never found out what happened. When my father found out, he was furious. I had disgraced the family—not just my parents but all my aunts and uncles and cousins. It was ridiculous, but that was how things like that were viewed and I was banished. By the time I got to New York I was two months along, and when I met your father . . . well he was sweet, and we really cared for each other, and he was willing to marry me. He was even excited to become a father. I liked him . . . a lot, actually. Never was there a kinder man in the world. So if you think about it I got pretty lucky. We both did."

Kay sat, clearly lost in thought.

"Mom, you know I love you. And I understand," Kay said. "Actually, that's not true . . . I could never understand what you went through. And I know that it has a lot to do with you going back to Italy now. You need to find some closure . . . I get it. But why the camino? Why do you have to walk all the way to Assisi?"

"I can't answer that question yet, honey. All I know is that I have to do it my way. It's like the final part of a very long journey, and I have to walk the rest, or crawl if I have to. Maybe I just need the time to acclimate before walking through that gate again. I don't know . . . it's just what I need."

"Dad was a pretty incredible guy, wasn't he?" Kay said as tears began to flow.

"He was the best," Anna said as she reached for her daughter's hand. "I hope you meet a man like him one day. Your first run was a bit of a scrub, wasn't it?" she said, making a face.

"Yeah, I guess it was," Kay said as she wiped the tears away. "But I've decided that if Penny and I ever let another man into our lives, he'll be a great one like Dad. Mystery man will have some pretty high standards to meet."

"Keep them. They'll serve you well."

Anna was startled back to the present when she suddenly felt the ground give way beneath her. Before she could regain her balance, she was slipping down a steep hill toward a shallow creek, the backpack ripped off her shoulders. Her arm reached out to break the fall and it twisted beneath her, sending her flipping forward, landing just short of the water. Pain shot up her arm and Anna pulled it close to her body, sitting upright and stifling a scream. She was sure her left wrist had to be broken.

The backpack was still halfway up the hill, but the thought of moving sent shock waves of pain through her body. Anna sat perfectly still for at least ten minutes before slowing shifting her body and beginning the slow and painful crawl back to the top, retrieving her pack and dragging it with her. Once she reached the trail, she saw a log and sat down, tears rolling down her cheek.

"What did you do?" Anna cried. "Why did you do that?"

It took several minutes for the pain to decrease to the point she could stand up again. She looked around hoping someone might be nearby, but realized she was alone. It took every ounce of courage she had to get the pack over her shoulder. She noticed the walking stick on the ground where she must have dropped it when she lost her footing. She gingerly reached down and took hold of the walking stick. Then she was walking again, much slower, afraid her journey had just come to an abrupt end.

Anna's pants were covered with mud and leaves, but none of that mattered. Her wrist was throbbing and she wasn't sure she would be able to continue. But what choice did she have? The other pilgrims were well ahead of her, and it might be morning before someone else came along. She carefully used one arm and a knee to open the guidebook to *Day Two* of the camino, relieved to see she would soon reach the Eremo di Cerbaiolo. Her goal had been to get all the way to Passo di Viamaggio, which was a normal day's walk. That's where the other pilgrims would be spending the night, but considering the pain she was feeling, she was unlikely to make it that far.

An hour later Anna saw the hermitage clinging to the hillside, and it filled her with new energy. Hopefully Chiara would be there and know something about broken bones. The aversion she might have felt spending the night at a hermitage was nothing compared to her need for care.

The last few steps that led to the medieval building were steep and perilous, but before long Anna had arrived. The front door was locked, so she knocked and waited. No one came. She tried again with the same result. She stepped back and looked around hoping to find someone, anyone to help her.

"*Buon giorno,*" a familiar voice said. Anna turned around and saw Giovanni sitting on a stone slab overlooking the valley below.

"Giovanni!" Anna cried. "I'm so happy to see you."

"And I am happy to see you as well," he said. Then he noticed the pain in Anna's eyes and how tightly she held her wrist to her body. "Oh no, something has happened. Did you fall?"

Anna walked closer, "Yes, I was stupid and fell down a hill. I think I broke my wrist."

"Come and let me take a look," he said as he stood up from his perch.

"Maybe we should find Chiara," Anna said. "I read about her in my guidebook."

"Well, I'm sorry to tell you this but Chiara left for Heaven in 2010," Giovanni said. "You must have an older version of the guidebook."

Anna looked around and wondered what her next move would be. If Chiara was no longer there, who was managing the Eremo? As if hearing her thoughts Giovanni said, "A caretaker comes and looks over the hermitage. But he isn't here right now, so why don't you let me have a look?"

Anna relaxed and let him examine her arm. It was painful, but his hands were so warm she didn't really mind. For a moment she had the feeling that something was happening, something strange and wonderful. But then she pushed the idea out of her mind, and as soon as she did the pain returned.

"It may be broken, I'm not sure," he said. "It's so good we found each other. We need to find a doctor but it might be hard before we reach Sansepolcro."

"That's not for another two days," Anna despairingly said to him. "I suppose I could hitchhike when I get to an actual road, but what about tonight? If the caretaker doesn't come where will we stay?"

"That's not a problem," Giovanni said with a grin. "I've been here many times and I know a secret. Come, let me show you."

He led Anna around to the back of the building until they came to a glassless window with wooden shutters. Giovanni pushed them open and told her to wait there. He climbed inside and disappeared, only to reappear seconds later through a door.

"You see? When God closes one door he always unlocks another. Oh, I'm sorry . . . I forgot—we are not to talk about God. I apologize."

"You can talk about God if you want," Anna said to him. "I just might not answer."

"Fair enough. Now follow me and I'll show you the way."

Giovanni led Anna into an old and stale-smelling hallway that didn't seem to have been used in centuries. Giovanni pushed open a door that led to what looked like a dining room and Anna followed him inside.

"I doubt he'll be back tonight," Giovanni said. "He never leaves much food behind, but there's always a little if you know where to look."

He opened a cupboard and took out several cans of soup. In the tin next to the cupboard he found a container with half a loaf of bread.

"Thank God you were here," Anna said to him. "I don't know what I would have done."

"It's very strange but I wasn't planning to stop. I wanted to go all the way to Passo di Viamaggio and find a guesthouse, but the sun was shining and I found such a nice spot to pray. Then you appeared, Anna."

"What about rooms?" Anna asked him.

"There are several rooms where pilgrims used to stay when the hermitage was open. Tonight it is open, with or without the help of the caretaker. But first let's get your wrist settled as best we can. I know there's a first-aid kit that will allow us to get your arm braced at the very least, as well as some pain meds. And then I can start making our meal."

"You have no idea what I would do for a cigarette right now," Anna said to him. He looked back at her with a mix of compassion and encouragement. "But I won't . . . not yet, anyway."

A short time later Anna's wrist was wrapped and braced against her chest and the pain was starting to dull with the help of the pain meds. She sat watching Giovanni ladle hot soup into bowls, which he served with sliced bread, and soon they were ready to share the simple meal he had prepared for them. Giovanni prayed over his food without words, then turned to Anna saying, "I'm glad that you don't believe in God."

"Why would you say that?" Anna asked, surprised.

"Because belief is such a weak energy, don't you think? People say they believe in God all the time, but their faith is never proven. If it's never put to the test then it means nothing. It would be better to have no belief and an open mind than an untested faith." He set down the slice of bread he was holding. "So here's my question to you, dear Anna: Do you have an open mind?"

"An open mind?" she repeated, clearly uncomfortable. "I think so. I have an open mind about many things."

"That's good, because I'm going to tell you something that I've never told anyone before, and it may shock you."

"Okay," Anna said, setting her soup spoon down to give him her full attention. "I think I'm ready."

"Contrary to what you might think," he said, clearing his throat, "I also do not believe in a God."

"That is a surprise. In fact, you're right—I'm shocked. Tell me more."

"As I said, I do not believe in a God . . . a God that is sitting up in Heaven somewhere judging people and looking down waiting for us to fail or sin. I do not believe in a God that loves one group of people at the expense of another just because they have different beliefs or different ways of loving the Divine. And I don't believe that there's only one path to the truth. I believe that there are many paths and they all lead to the same place—unconditional love. So no, I do not believe in a God. But there's one thing I need to add."

"This is really fascinating, so please continue," Anna said.

"I do not believe in a God—I believe in ONLY God."

"What does that mean?"

"It's very simple," Giovanni continued. "I believe that God is the only thing that exists. The problem is in the word *God*. We imagine that there's something out there separate from us or higher than us, and we're doing our best to get to him."

"Now you're really freaking me out."

"No, listen to me . . . I'm not trying to freak you out, only tell you what I think is true. There's no separate God simply because God is EVERYWHERE. Maybe I use the word *God* while another person uses the words *Great Spirit* or *Allah* . . . but none of that matters. God is not a word or a concept. God is the Ultimate Reality that is everywhere at the same time."

"And how does that sit with your Catholic beliefs?" Anna asked him, picking up her spoon to resume eating her soup.

"Very well, I think. The word *catholic* means 'universal.' Did you know that? But for many centuries it's been changed to mean something else. And Jesus's main message was to love one another just as God loves us. It's that simple. So the closest we can come to the reality some people call God is to love one another without conditions."

Satisfied with his point, Giovanni picked up his bread and dipped it into his soup before taking a bite.

"You make it sound so simple," Anna said, watching him dig into his meal.

"It is simple . . . but people always make it seem so complicated. My motto is 'teach only love, for that is what you are.' In other words, I'm not here to teach or learn complicated theological concepts but to simply keep my heart always open to love. In my experience, that's the one who is closest to God."

"But you do believe there's something out there that created us and made good and evil and all that?" Anna asked.

"Yes and no," said Giovanni, taking another spoonful of soup. "We were created—we can both agree about that, yes? We exist. Whether we were created by millions of years of proteins and DNA bouncing off each other or by a single force of energy some people call God means very little to me. I have no idea how it all works. But I know it works. We're sitting here together in this little hermitage having a lovely dinner, so something is working that we can't fully comprehend. I had the impulse to stay here and not go to Passo di Viamaggio, and then you show up with a hurt wrist. You can say that it's all accidental, or you can believe everything happens for a reason. I believe there's a reason for everything that happens. I call that God."

"You are a real surprise," Anna said to him.

"The Poverello saw God in everything, not just in the church or in the Bible. Those things are important, but they can't take the place of seeing God everywhere. Whenever he came across a slip of paper with random words on it he treated it as something sacred because the same words had once been used to describe God or express someone's love of the Divine. That may seem strange to us now, or even extreme, but it reminds us of something really important—God is everywhere and in everything."

Anna was surprised she didn't feel a negative reaction to his words. Giovanni was presenting a "God" she could relate to, perhaps for the first time in her life. And the fact that it was coming from someone so young intrigued her. This vibrant young Italian had captured her attention.

After finishing their meal, Giovanni found a pile of wood stacked by the kitchen door and lit a fire in a small fireplace. The glow of the embers and the sound of the crackling wood mesmerized Anna, pulling her into a deep chamber she didn't know existed before that moment. Here she was, alone in the middle of nowhere, with a man she barely knew, and yet she realized that she trusted Giovanni completely. The thought felt foreign, almost unwelcome. Secrets were swimming through her mind, the kind of secrets she never imagined she would tell, especially to someone she had just met. She watched Giovanni stoke the fire and had the feeling he was doing the same to her heart.

"I have something to tell you," she said hesitantly. The words came slow and vulnerable. "I'm not really an American. Well, I guess I am . . . I'm a citizen and all that, but I wasn't born an American."

"You're Italian," he said. "I already knew that."

"How did you know?"

"Your accent," he grinned at her. "The way you say certain words. Very Italian."

"I was seventeen when I left for the US, and this is the first time I've been back."

"Why now? You didn't want to come back before?"

Anna looked at the fire wondering how much more she should reveal.

"Not really. I put it all behind me. I have a daughter and a granddaughter back in Portland. But for some reason this felt like the right time. And if I told you what happened you probably wouldn't believe me."

"Do I look like the kind of person who wouldn't believe a story about fate?"

"You think it's fate that brought me back here? The truth is I was hit on the head by a book about the Camino of St. Francis. It's called *On the Road with St. Francis*."

"By Angela Seracchioli," Giovanni said.

"Yes, exactly. Do you know her?"

"I know her book. Please go on with your story."

"As I said I was hit on the head by her book. Strange as that sounds it's the truth. I was walking through a bookstore in Portland when it fell and hit me right on the noggin. One thing led to another and here I am. You can't make up this stuff."

"Who do you think pushed that book?" he asked her.

"Don't get all mystical on me," she laughed. "I looked for every possible explanation but couldn't find one. But that doesn't mean it was an angel."

"Maybe, maybe not," he said. "All I know is that you're here now and that's what's important. Whether an angel pushed it or a twelve-year-old boy playing a trick on you, it brought you back to Italy."

"And then I meet you," she said. "How do you fit into all this, anyway?"

"What do you mean?"

"I don't really know, only that it's all so strange. This handsome young Italian shows up out of nowhere and gets me thinking about things I haven't considered in decades. Maybe it was you who pushed that book off the shelf," accused Anna, jokingly.

Giovanni laughed, holding his hands up in defeat. "You caught me, Anna. I saw you walking down the aisle and said 'This woman needs to get hit on the head by a book about St. Francis.'"

"It wouldn't surprise me," she said smiling. "You've got my head all turned around so anything's possible."

They talked for another hour until Anna felt her body giving way. Giovanni showed her to one of the guest rooms and stood at the door before saying good night.

"Remember, Anna, nothing happens by accident. We're all here for a reason. The trick is to find out what that reason is."

"Good night, Giovanni."

"Good night, sweet Anna," he said, closing the door.

5

TRUE CREATIVITY

Giovanni and Anna arrived at Passo di Viamaggio by eleven the next morning. Anna's wrist had swollen overnight and the alarming ache left her with few options. She needed to find a doctor, yet the tiny village of Passo di Viamaggio was hardly more than a small collection of houses. The possibility of finding a doctor seemed remote, and if her wrist was indeed broken it might need to be reset before it had a chance to start healing out of place.

"It's hopeless," she said to him. "We'll never find a doctor here."

"We are on the camino," Giovanni said. "Everything we need will be provided."

Just then a young woman holding a baby was passing on the other side of the road. Anna waited to the side as Giovanni stopped her to ask if there were any clinics in the town. Anna could tell from his expression that the answer was yes. The woman pointed back in the direction they had just come, then returned to her walk.

"I have very good news," he said when he came to her side. "There is a chiropractor from Sansepolcro who has a country home here."

"A chiropractor?" She said desperately. "I don't need a chiropractor . . . I need a real doctor."

"But he is a doctor . . . a doctor of chiropractic medicine. Unfortunately, he's all we have unless we want to keep walking to Sansepolcro, but that's another twenty-four kilometers, and it's probably the most difficult part of the camino. I suggest we stay here tonight and get an early start in the morning."

"I don't need my back cracked, I need someone to take an X-ray of my arm to see if it's broken," grumbled Anna, already resigned and turning in the direction the women had pointed.

"Maybe he won't need to X-ray your arm to see if it's broken," he said brightly. "And we're always guided in the right direction if we follow the signs."

"There you go with that spiritual stuff again," she said, though her tone was playful rather than sharp.

Five minutes later they came to a small house surrounded by an ancient stone wall, and Anna noticed smoke coming from the chimney. The house fit in well with the picturesque landscape, but she wasn't optimistic about her chances of getting the help she needed. They knocked on the door, and a thin man around sixty years old answered, introducing himself as Dr. Marconi.

"How can I help you?" he asked as they stepped inside. Anna watched as he looked back and forth between Giovanni and herself, clearly confused by the pair.

"We are pilgrims walking the Camino of St. Francis," Giovanni said as they sat down in the doctor's living room. "Yesterday as my friend was walking through the forest . . ."

"I think I broke my wrist when I fell," she interrupted. The pain was starting to really annoy her.

Marconi was clearly confused and continued scanning between the two.

"You fell and your wrist is broken . . . and I am to do what?"

Anna reached for her backpack and was ready to leave but Giovanni stopped her.

"We understand that you are not a medical doctor," Giovanni answered. "But we also know that a pilgrimage like ours is filled with challenges to test our resolve. This is one such challenge. We're hoping you have an X-ray machine."

"This is my country home so there is no X-ray machine," the doctor said. "But maybe I can have a look and we'll see if there is any care I can offer."

"Now you're catching on," Anna said sarcastically. Giovanni nudged her under the table.

"Thank you. That would save us having to walk to Sansepolcro to find a doctor," Giovanni said in a happy tone. "And one more thing, doctor. . . ." Giovanni shifted his weight in the chair and looked deep into the doctor's eyes. "Your work has been very important to many people, more than you know. It's easy to feel alone sometimes, but you are anything but alone. There are more people thinking about you right now than you can imagine."

The chiropractor sat in shocked silence. Anna looked at Giovanni as if he had lost his mind.

"What in the world are you talking about?" she whispered at him.

The doctor stood up and turned toward the window.

"Sometimes I do feel alone," Dr. Marconi said pensively.

After a time, his shoulders visibly relaxed and he turned back around. "I hope you're right, young man. I hope you're right."

With that he motioned for Anna to follow him into the next room while Giovanni waited. Anna turned and looked at him one last time as if searching for a clue, then followed the doctor.

An hour later Anna and Giovanni were back on the road leaving Passo di Viamaggio, Anna's wrist tightly wrapped in a temporary cast.

"At least it wasn't broken," she said to him. "Now I just need to stay on my feet and resist the urge to summersault down hills."

"We were very fortunate to find Dr. Marconi," Giovanni said. "Did you notice the picture on the table, a picture of a dark-haired woman?"

"Yes, I did. I assumed it's his wife."

"Was his wife," Giovanni said. "She passed away three weeks ago."

"How do you know that?"

"When you were getting your X-ray an older woman came into the office to leave some food. She told me. She said it has been very hard for him and that he felt very alone. Maybe that's the reason we were sent to him."

Anna stopped and looked at him suspiciously.

"You said those things to him before you spoke to anyone," she said. "So how did you know any of that?"

Giovanni shrugged his shoulders playfully.

"As I said before, we are always given what we need on the camino, but we are also given to others who are in need. Does that make sense?"

"Not at all," she told Giovanni. "I didn't hurt my wrist just so we could show up at that man's house. It doesn't work that way."

"Are you sure about that?" Giovanni said with a smile. "Every thought is a prayer and every desire is a benediction. Those prayers go out into the Universe and are sometimes received by angels and sometimes even by people like you and me. He needed someone to remind him that he is loved because his heart's broken. Maybe we were the ones who heard his prayer."

"What I want to know is how you knew his wife had been killed before anyone told you?"

Anna searched his eyes for an answer. He finally smiled and said:

"The woman I stopped on the road . . . she was holding a baby . . . do you remember?"

"Yes, of course I do."

"She told me. It's as simple as that."

Anna looked at him skeptically, wondering if he was telling her the truth.

"I may have been on the other side of the road when you talked to her but I was close enough to hear what she said. I don't remember her saying anything like that."

"All we need to remember is that we're given what we need when we need it. Always. But we have to be ready to listen. That's the key."

Then he started walking again, and Anna was left standing alone at the side of the road. After a few seconds she surrendered and turned to follow.

Giovanni led Anna to a guesthouse called La Casetta di Ca' la Fonte on the edge of town where they would spend the night. Parked outside the hotel were at least a dozen motorcycles with men and women who had been touring the Italian countryside. Giovanni greeted each of them as if they were close friends, though Anna was sure they had never met. One of them asked Giovanni if he would like to ride with them, but he declined, saying:

"My feet are meant for the earth, and so I walk everywhere I go."

They were amazed by his words and his simple life. Anna watched all this from a distance and thought how lucky she was to have met him, though another part of her wondered if it was too good to be true. He seemed to fall out of the sky, and though his words often unsettled her, she was happy to have such a companion.

𝝉

The next morning, Anna and Giovanni entered the Alpe della Luna nature reserve and, while standing atop one of the hills, Giovanni pointed at a two-hundred-meter-high ravine of marl and sandstone that jutted against the sky in an almost vertical slope.

"Anna, tell me if the shape of that ravine reminds you of anything."

Anna looked at the landscape but couldn't see what he meant. The slopes were covered with dense and spectacular vegetation made of age-old beech trees, as well as holly trees and colorful crocuses, cyclamens, and matgrass, but the shape did not stir anything in her mind.

"Do you see the shape of the crescent moon?" he finally asked her. "It is the reason for its name—Alpe della Luna or Mountain of the Moon. There is a story of St. Francis that relates to this place, though very few people have ever heard it. Alpe della Luna was part of the inspiration to write his most famous prayer."

"Do you mean 'The Prayer of St. Francis'?" Anna asked as she slipped the pack off her shoulders, then leaned over to rub her aching calves with her good arm. "I remember it from when I was a child. 'Lord make me an instrument of your peace.'"

"Actually, that prayer was not written by St. Francis, though it's so often attributed to him."

Anna was taken aback by this news.

"Are you sure?" she said. "I see it everywhere, and it always has his name attached."

"It captures his spirit," Giovanni explained, "but it actually came from a French magazine called *The Little Bell*. At one point there was a holy card made with the prayer on one side and a picture of Francesco on the other, and that's how it became known as 'The Prayer of St. Francis.' No, I'm talking about the real prayer he wrote called 'The Canticle of the Creatures.' It was written at the very end of his life—about the sun and the moon, the water and the air, and all the creatures that praise God through their very existence. Francesco stood here looking out over the vast forest and seeing the shape of the moon made him think about the church."

"The Catholic church?" Anna said with a moan. "Please don't go there."

"It's just a story, Anna. To Francesco the church was meant to reflect the light of God—not BE the light. Unfortunately, religion has often been used to consolidate power or influence, and the Catholic church is no exception. In Francesco's time it definitely wasn't an exception. It was the end of the Dark Ages, a very difficult time for Europe and the church. Popes had been treated like kings for hundreds of years and the spirit of Christ was nearly lost. But there was a new movement about to begin, and when Francesco stood here in this spot it became very clear to him."

"How do you know all this?" Anna asked, standing straight again. "Your insights seem more personal than something you read in a book."

"So many books have been written about the Poverello," Giovanni told her, "some of them not long after he left the earth. Many of his brothers knew about this place because Francesco often told them about it. He had a great epiphany here, when everything became so clear to him. He realized that salvation would only come if people dedicated themselves to imitating Christ—by becoming poor, as he was poor, and desiring only the riches of Heaven. This would counteract the opulence of the church and initiate a great movement that would help the church and the whole world reflect the light of God once again."

"How is that different from today?" Anna asked. "The church is still opulent and more concerned with riches and power than serving the poor."

"Yes, but look what's happening right now. What name did the new pope choose?"

"He chose the name Francis," she said.

"Do you think that's an accident? Of course not. Eight hundred years ago Francesco's influence helped lead Europe out of the Dark Ages into a period of great inspiration and light. Do you know what that time was called?"

"The Renaissance, of course."

"That's correct. The Renaissance. Some of the greatest art in history came from that period—a time of amazing inspiration and creativity. And now here we are today, in a different kind of dark age. Humanity has never been more focused on materialism and worldly power. And then a pope comes along who sees the need for a new era of service—and he calls himself Francis. Do you see what I mean? Yes, things are very dark right now, in the church and in the world, but there is a great light that is beginning to dawn, and it was here in this spot that it first took root."

"All because he saw a cliff shaped like the moon," Anna said. "It seems like a stretch to me."

"Maybe if I shared the prayer with you, maybe then you'd understand what he meant."

Anna recoiled at the suggestion of prayer. "I'm not very interested in praying, even with you," she said stiffly.

"Then think of it more as a poem," Giovanni said. "Many people consider it one of the great nature poems of the era."

"Fine," she said, "go ahead and share your prayer."

Giovanni threw his pack to the ground then closed his eyes, as if centering himself for a performance. He opened them again and, looking to the sky, began reciting the prayer with great reverence.

> Most High, all-powerful, good Lord,
> Yours are the praises, the glory, and the honor, and all
>   blessing,
> To You alone, Most High, do they belong,
>   and no human is worthy to mention Your name.
>
> Praised be You, my Lord, with all Your creatures,
>   especially Sir Brother Sun,
> Who is the day and through whom You give us light.
> And he is beautiful and radiant with great splendor,
>   and bears a likeness of You, Most High One.
>
> Praised be You, my Lord, through Sister Moon and the
>   stars, in heaven You formed them clear and precious
>   and beautiful.
>
> Praised be You, my Lord, through Brother Wind, and
>   through the air, cloudy and serene, and every kind of
>   weather, through whom You give sustenance to Your
>   creatures.
>
> Praised be You, my Lord, through Sister Water, who
>   is very useful and humble and precious and chaste.
>
> Praised be You, my Lord, through Brother Fire,
>   through whom You light the night, and he is beauti-
>   ful and playful and robust and strong.

Praised be You, my Lord, through our Sister Mother
Earth, who sustains and governs us, and who pro-
duces various fruit with colored flowers and herbs.

Praised be You, my Lord, through those who give
pardon for Your love, and bear infirmity and trib-
ulation. Blessed are those who endure in peace
for by You, Most High, shall they be crowned.

Praise and bless my Lord and give Him thanks and
serve Him with great humility.

Anna was deeply moved by the prayer but something in her didn't
want Giovanni to know. Whatever she was protecting herself from was
fading before her eyes. She turned away from him to pick up her walking stick from where she had leaned it against a tree and began walking
again.

"Nice performance," she said over her shoulder. "But you know me—
too many references to God throw me off."

"Maybe you're right, Anna." He replied as he fell into step with her.
"I know it's not something you want to talk or think about. You must
have been terribly wounded by the church."

Anna wanted to lash out at the comment. Of course the church had
wounded her. Being raised in Assisi was like a prison sentence for anyone wanting to stretch in new directions—especially with a father who
thought he was related to St. Francis. Obviously, his daughter had to be
an example of conservative religious values, but his stifling expectations
had only pushed her further away from her family, her town, and her
religion. Then she was shunned and sent away because she didn't fit his
image of the chaste Italian virgin.

"I think I've had enough of St. Francis for one camino," she said as
she stopped on the path, planting her walking stick firmly in the ground.
"It's great that you're such an expert, but every time I hear one of your

stories an alarm goes off inside of me." Then she looked down at the ground and said, "Maybe it's better that I walk alone like I planned."

Giovanni hesitated, as if searching for the right thing to say. He looked at Anna with eyes filled with compassion and humility. "You're right," he finally said. "I've been talking too much and not listening enough. If you want to walk on your own I will understand, but first, I'd like to ask you a question."

"Okay," she said, "but only one."

"Where in Italy did you come from? I think I know already but I'd love to hear it from you."

"What difference does that make?" she said. "There's very little of that town left in me now. I left a long time ago and never looked back."

"You never looked back, yes, but I believe it's one of the reasons you're here now. If you push something away hard enough it always comes back to you. Here you are walking in the footsteps of the Poverello even though you don't believe in God and have every reason to be angry."

Anna felt vulnerable and considered walking away, not answering the question, and leaving Giovanni behind forever. She never planned on making friends on the walk, certainly not one with such a penetrating gaze who seemed to know more about her than he should. And yet, the thought of leaving and walking on her own filled Anna's heart with a sadness she didn't expect.

"Fine, I'll tell you," Anna said to him. "I'm from Assisi, the home of your beloved Poverello. He's been under my fingernail my entire life, like a stale smell I can't get out of my clothes no matter how many times I wash them. And here's the funniest part—my family name is Bernardone—the same as St. Francis. My father always told me we're related, though I've never believed it for a second. He used to tell tourists he was St. Francis's second cousin twenty-five times removed and they would take pictures with him and tell their families back home that they met a relative of St. Francis. What a scam."

"It's not a common name," Giovanni told her.

"I knew three other Bernardones in Assisi," she said to him, "but that doesn't mean we're all related to St. Francis. It was more of a burden than anything else. People expected me to live up to an ideal that had nothing to do with me. The harder I tried the more trouble I got into."

"What did your father do for a living?" Giovanni asked. "I'm sure he didn't just have pictures taken."

"You probably won't believe me. He owned a fabric store."

"Just like Francesco's father," Giovanni laughed.

"Exactly. I think he opened the shop just to keep the illusion alive. He had a picture at the entrance comparing himself with Pietro Bernardone, St. Francis's father. Like I said, it was all a ruse."

Anna started walking again, clearly uncomfortable with the conversation. Giovanni stayed a step behind, allowing her time to experience whatever was happening within her. The sound of Anna's walking stick thumped on the dirt path. She looked one last time at the moon-shaped ravine, then set her gaze directly in front of herself.

"Maybe this is not the best time to tell you this," Giovanni called out before she got too far ahead, "but I am also from Assisi."

Anna stopped and turned around. "You're kidding. Why didn't you say anything before?"

"It didn't seem important until now," he said.

"How many times have you walked this camino?" Anna asked him.

"It would be difficult to say," Giovanni said with a smile. "My life is very different than before. My parents are no longer alive, and the rest of my family has been scattered, but Assisi still calls to me. I've been walking this path most of my life."

"Tell me more about your family," she said as she walked back toward him.

"It was very typical," Giovanni told her. "When I was a teenager I wanted all the normal things—to be popular and have money. But none of them made me happy. That was something I only found through giving my life away to serve others."

"Maybe you should have become a priest." She said to him, the thought sounding strange as it came from her mouth.

"I did think about it," Giovanni continued, "but even that felt constraining. I wanted to be like the birds of the air or the lilies of the field, and that's when I started walking the camino. I always meet interesting people, just like you."

"I doubt you've ever met anyone like me before," she said, "a lady who doesn't even believe in God walking to a town she hasn't seen in forty years."

"You'd be surprised at the people I meet," he said.

"What happened to your family, if you don't mind me asking."

"We don't speak anymore but they're with me in spirit. My father was in business, and my mother was a beautiful woman who tried to understand me, but in the end she couldn't. They've been gone for a long time now. I never had a great relationship with my father, but I loved him very much. He didn't even like my name."

"What do you mean?" Anna asked.

"My mother chose a name, but my father . . . he had a different idea."

"Brothers and sisters?" she asked him.

"I don't really know where they are." Then he smiled and joked, "Who knows, maybe we're related."

"Wouldn't that be funny?" she laughed, finally pushing away the tension she was holding in her body. "I think I would have like being related to you, Giovanni. Now let's stop hanging around and get home—both of us."

Giovanni smiled and stepped up next to Anna, and they were walking again.

6

A BED OF STONE

Several hours later, the two companions arrived at the Eremo di Montecasale, a hermitage where St. Francis had stayed when he was traveling to the Adriatic, to set sail for the Holy Land in 1213. In the chapel, Giovanni pointed to an ancient-looking statue of Mary, wearing a crown and holding her infant son Jesus.

"What do you think of her?" Giovanni asked Anna.

"Who? Mary?"

"Yes, what do you think of Mary?"

Anna hesitated before answering. Her first impulse was to say that she didn't think about her at all. But that wasn't true. As a child she'd had a deep and particular (if innocent and naïve) love for the Blessed Mother. Anna's mother had told her that Mary was always watching over her, and she believed it. Anna could remember nights when her mother had rocked her in her arms, telling her that Mary held a special place in their family, even closer than an aunt or cousin.

"When he came through here, St. Francis found this statue of Mary holding Jesus in the ruins of the castle," Giovanni said.

"My mother told me she was my guardian," Anna said to Giovanni. "That's one thing I never understood about being Catholic, how Mary is put on the same level as Jesus."

"What if you put everyone on the same level as Jesus?" Giovanni asked.

She turned to him, surprised and exasperated all at once.

"What does that mean? I thought you're still religious."

"I'm not religious at all," he said, "at least not in the usual way. I was raised Catholic, of course, but now I'm more spiritual than religious. I love all the different ways people love God."

"That's what people say now, isn't it? 'Spiritual but not religious,' even in their online dating profiles."

"Here's the difference," Giovanni continued. "People usually believe that following a particular religion is going to give them answers. I'm not looking for the right answers. I'm looking for the right questions. When you think you already have the answer then you're not open to true inspiration, even when it's right in front of you. So once again, what if you put everyone at the same level as Jesus, or saw everyone you meet as Christ?"

"But people can't live up to it. Most people will disappoint you."

"Everyone will disappoint you if you expect them to act a certain way or do certain things. But what if you didn't expect anything? What if your only goal is to see them as God sees them?"

"We're back to God then?"

"Let me change that. What if you saw everyone through the eyes of love? I believe that's what God does—sees everyone as loving and lovable."

"What about people who commit evil?" Anna asked. "Surely they're not lovable."

"Yesterday I said that God is love, do you remember? If that's what God is, then is it possible for God to be unloving? The sun shines on the good and the evil alike. It doesn't block its light from people who commit evil acts."

"What about Hell?" Anna asked Giovanni, thinking she found a wire to trip him.

"Are you asking if evil people go to Hell?"

"Yes, that's what I'm asking."

"I don't have an answer to that question," he said. "I like to stick with the simplest truth I can understand: God is love. What happens after that isn't my concern. My only job is to imitate God by seeing everyone as Christ."

"I thought Catholics believe that Jesus was the only son of God."

"He is," Giovanni said to her, then after a long pause he added, "and so are you."

"All right, now you're confusing me."

"It's better to be confused by love than to think you understand it. You can't understand love with your mind, but if you open your heart and try to see every person you meet as Jesus, or Mary, then a door opens inside you, and you learn the greatest lesson you can ever learn in this world."

"And what is that?" Anna asked.

"That love is one."

"Love is one. What does that mean?"

"That's what you're here to find out, Anna. Come with me. I want to show you something." Then Giovanni walked through a small door at the side of the chapel and Anna followed him.

A short distance inside they came to a series of stone steps that led up to a tiny slab of rock. Anna saw a small drawing of St. Francis on the rock and flowers left by visitors.

"This is where St. Francis slept when he was here," Giovanni told her, "on that little slab of stone. It reminded him that he was homeless in this world. We're all poor no matter how much money we have. We're also rich and abundant no matter how little money we have. Do you see what I'm saying? Francesco understood this so he chose to live as close to the earth as he could."

"If you ask me, he was a masochist," Anna said to him.

"Not at all," said a voice from behind them. A small Franciscan friar who looked to be about seventy entered the room. Giovanni's eyes lit up.

"Padre Nicola," he said, wrapping his arms around the friar.

"It's so good to see you, Giovanni. I see you're doing my job for me again."

"This is my friend Anna," Giovanni said, "from Portland, in the US."

"Portland, Oregon," said Anna, reaching out her hand but Padre Nicola opened his arms and embraced her.

"Welcome, Anna," he said to her. "We are blessed you came."

"Padre Nicola has lived here for many years," Giovanni said to her. "He can tell you more about Francesco than anyone I know."

"I hear stories then I repeat them, that's all," the priest said. "But they never tell the whole story. For that you have to experience it for yourself. Please, go up to the top and lie down where St. Francis used to sleep. Then you'll understand what I mean."

Anna hesitated and looked at Giovanni.

"It's okay, Anna," Giovanni said to her. "See what you think."

Anna climbed the steps that led to the stone slab. At first she didn't know if she should reach down and touch the spot or actually lie down. She looked down and the priest gave her a reassuring nod. She knelt, guarding her wrist as she did, feeling the ground with her hand and then lowering herself until she was on her back.

At first she didn't feel anything but the cold rock beneath her, but then . . . was it her imagination or was there a buzzing feeling in her heart? The buzzing increased until her entire body filled with a light that seemed brighter than the sun. When she felt like sitting up she did, and the sensation stopped.

"What did you feel?" Nicola called up.

Anna stood looking at them, trying not to show how shaken she felt. What had just happened? She refused to believe that a saint who had slept on a slab of rock eight hundred years ago would cause a reaction inside her. Was it some kind of strange hypnosis, the result of walking beside Giovanni for the last two days? But it felt so real and there was no way Anna could deny it.

"Nothing," she lied. "I didn't feel anything."

τ

Padre Nicola served them a light meal and an hour later Anna and Giovanni sat together on a patio with a spectacular view of the valley below. The sun was sinking behind the hills and by then Anna had rationalized her way around the phenomenon she felt on the stone bed, convinced that it was all in her mind.

"I don't get you," she said to Giovanni. "You hike back and forth between here and Assisi, God knows how many times, picking up old ladies who don't even believe in God. Why? There were at least fifteen other people leaving La Verna the same day we were, and who knows how many behind us? Why not walk with them—people closer to your own age?"

"Because you were hurt and needed my help," he said matter-of-factly.

"There has to be more to it than that. You could have helped me get to a doctor and then been on your way. Why are you still here?"

"It's a good question," Giovanni said. "It's true, I could have left you at Dr. Marconi's and continued walking. But something told me to stay."

"What was it?" she asked. "Definitely not my positive attitude! And I'm only slowing you down."

"Maybe you remind me of someone . . . who I haven't seen in a very long time."

"Like who? I'm serious, Giovanni . . . I'd really like to know. I love walking with you in spite of all your God talk. Then something will come out of your mouth that surprises me to no end. I can't figure you out."

Giovanni looked out over the landscape that was beginning to disappear before their eyes. Then he looked back at her and said, "Look at those hills behind us. In two days we've walked along paths that have connected these villages for hundreds of years, long before there were roads and cars. It's only from here that we can appreciate how far we've traveled. If you look at the hill there in the middle, La Verna is somewhere on the other side. It's the same with our lives: you look back and see all the markers that made you who you are—the challenges you've encountered, both good and bad. They all brought you here—to this moment. And it's in this moment that you get to make a choice—to either continue living as you did before or make new choices."

"None of that answers my question," Anna said to him.

"I'm walking with you because I get to see the camino for the first time, just as you do. And along the way we learn new lessons and make new choices. We only know that our lives will never be the same. That's why I walk these ancient paths—because I get to see them for the first time through you."

"I did feel something when I was lying on that stone slab," she admitted. "And I don't know why I didn't want to confess it to Father Nicola either."

"Tell me what you felt," Giovanni said quietly.

"I don't think I can. It was energy. To tell you the truth, it scared me."

"Because you didn't believe things like that happen? Especially not to you?"

"I don't know if I believe anything happened at all," she told him. "You've been weaving some kind of spell over my mind, all your talk about St. Francis."

"Here's another way to think about it," Giovanni said. "People have been coming to this hermitage for hundreds of years, and they all lay down on that stone slab just like you did. Maybe it wasn't St. Francis's energy you felt but the hopes and desires of all the other people who came before you—some with strong faith and others with no faith. So my question, dear Anna, is what do you believe?"

"I believe it's time for me to find my room and get some sleep," she said.

"You can do better than that. You don't believe it was the energy of St. Francis. Maybe it was you. Maybe you were feeling something inside yourself that you've refused to see until now."

"What does that mean?"

"No one walks the camino for no reason," Giovanni continued. "You have a reason and it's very personal."

"I have no idea why I'm doing this," she said. "My daughter thinks I'm crazy and she's probably right. A book falls off a shelf and hits me on the head, and the next thing I know I'm here talking to you. Why does everything need to be so mysterious?"

"The Universe *is* mysterious," Giovanni said. "It's all a mystery, and we're just doing our best to find our place in it."

"All I can say is that I felt something, but I can't say what it was. If you figure it out please tell me, but until then I'm going to get some sleep."

As if on cue, Padre Nicola came around the corner holding a towel, washcloth, and key. "It isn't much, but we're happy to have you spend the night with us," he said. "Anyone Giovanni brings is family. If you want to make a donation to the eremo that's okay, but nothing is required."

Anna stood up and smiled at the priest, then took the pile from his hands. "I'm very grateful, Padre. I think it's time for me to get some rest. I'll see you both in the morning."

Resting in her tiny bedroom that night, Anna thought about the energy she felt lying on the stone bed. Was it really just her imagination, or was there another, even more mysterious explanation? The idea that St. Francis himself had left his imprint on the slab of rock was too far of a leap. Even Giovanni's explanation felt too mystical to her. *People don't leave their energy behind, no matter how strong their faith is.* The fact that she was wondering how it was possible for her to feel something told her one of two things: either she was losing her mind or there was something going on she couldn't understand with her rational mind. But did she want to understand? Maybe it was better to leave such questions alone, to push them as far away as possible. Because the other possibility—that there was something much more mysterious at play—was even more frightening.

She closed her eyes and found herself drifting away from the Eremo di Montecasale, away from the Camino of St. Francis, back in time to a familiar house she hadn't visited in decades, not even in her dreams.

"You're never going to make anything of your life if you keep thinking that way," Anna's father said to her. "Maybe if we had more children it would have been easier for you to find your place."

She was seventeen, and tensions in the Bernardone house had reached a fevered pitch. Months earlier Anna decided she wouldn't play by her father's rules, and that led to a dramatic and uncomfortable turn.

"And where is my place, Papa? Am I supposed to sit around in the house all day like Mama, watching you make a fool out of us?"

A rough hand came crashing against the side of Anna's face, sending her off her chair onto the stone floor where she remained, unable and unwilling to move.

"How dare you?" he said. "How dare you speak to me like that? This family is all we have—and this town is what gives us our history."

"A history that isn't even real," she said into her hands, afraid to expose herself again. "It's all make believe and you know it."

Anna's mother was suddenly there, shielding her. "That's enough," she said. "Stop acting like this, both of you!"

His wife rarely challenged his authority but he remained unmoved. It was time for his daughter to fall in line. To throw the family's reputation into the dirt—it was inexcusable. In a town like Assisi reputation is everything and history is like a coat passed down from one generation to the next. Over the years and decades it grows threadbare, but after a stitch or two it's right back to normal. Anna's attitude threatened everything he believed in.

"I'm done with both of you," he said, then slammed the door as he left.

"Why does he treat me like that?" Anna asked, weeping into her mother's arms.

"Because he thinks you don't respect him, or the family."

Anna sat up and focused fierce eyes on her mother. "What is there to respect, Mama? It's all I hear about—the family history—and I don't believe any of it."

"But it's important to him," she said to her daughter. "If you love him, and I know you do, then you'll give him that gift."

But it was not a gift Anna could offer, not then, and not ever. She stood up and wiped away her tears, then followed her father through the door.

Later that night she met a young man visiting his family from another part of Italy. He was beautiful, and he seemed to like her. It was the kind of attention she had craved at the time, not knowing her life soon would be forever changed because of it.

The sound of church bells and sunlight casting patterns on Anna's bed brought her back to the eremo. She sat up and looked at the nightstand, spotting the piece of paper she had been carrying since leaving La Verna. She opened it up and read, *Renaldo B., Via Eremo delle Carceri #5, Assisi.* Then she folded it again and placed it in a small pocket in her backpack.

"Am I chasing you or are you chasing me?" she asked the empty air.

The small dining room was empty, and Anna wondered if she had missed breakfast. Maybe she was early. She walked onto the balcony where she and Giovanni had sat the previous evening and looked out over the landscape. Breathtaking. Then she spotted a modern looking statue of St. Francis gazing out over the valley as if lost in deep meditation. How had she not seen this before? The balcony was not well lit at night so it must have been hiding in the shadows. She walked over to the statue and put her hand on its shoulder.

"Well, Francesco, maybe it's time you and I had a little chat," she said. "It's probably going to be a bit one-sided since, after all, you're just a statue. Nevertheless, there are a few things I need to share."

Anna sat down so she was level with the statue, looking straight into its eyes. She hesitated, looking around to make sure she was alone, then cleared her throat and said: "What the hell happened, anyway? I couldn't live up to you and I couldn't live up to that town. And I especially couldn't live up to him, no matter what I said or did. I guess you could say that in the end I got the better end of the deal. I have Kay and Penny to thank for that, and I lived a good life in the US which probably wouldn't have happened if I'd stayed here." She reached out and put her hand on St. Francis's knee. "So why, you might be asking, am I going back now? I wish I had the answer to that question, cousin. Maybe I just needed to see it one last time before I put this chapter to rest, or maybe something more . . . we'll see. All I know is that I'm here so I might as well make the best of it."

Then she leaned in close, as if she didn't want anyone else to hear the conversation.

"But there is one more thing—this Giovanni guy. He has a lot of insight into you. Any chance you can tell me anything about him? It's like he fell from the sky and—I have to admit—I like him. So if there's anything you can tell me I'd be grateful."

She leaned in closer as if he was about to say something, then she leaned back and stood up. "I didn't think so. Just talking to stone, as usual."

Anna stood up and walked back through the door. She was still alone and out of nowhere she suddenly worried that Giovanni had left without her. Had she offended him to the point that he decided to walk the rest of the camino alone? They had only been walking together for two days, but the thought of continuing without him filled her with despair. But why? The plan had always been to walk alone. The thought of having to deal with another person, especially a young man who wouldn't stop talking about God and St. Francis, was her worst nightmare before she began the journey. But in two short days he had woven himself into her heart, and she hadn't realized it till that very moment. If he was gone . . . how would she tell him how grateful she was?

"Hello, is there anyone here?"

Anna's voice echoed off the ancient hermitage walls, but no other sound returned to greet her. Padre Nicola was the only friar she had met, but there must be more. Even hermits had to come out of their cells to eat. Anna felt a heavy weight descending over her and did her best to push it away, but it was surprisingly strong. If it grew any stronger she didn't know what she would do.

She walked through an open door and began ascending the stone staircase that led to St. Francis's stone bed. She looked at the spot wondering if she should move closer or keep a safe distance. No explanation Giovanni had offered about the energy she had experienced the previous day had helped calm her fear. Part of her wanted to grab her backpack and run out of the hermitage with or without Giovanni, but another deeper part wanted to climb the stairs and lie flat on the stone once more.

Chances were she would feel nothing and would conclude it was all in her imagination. But what if she did feel something? Was she ready to repeat the experience from the previous day and risk her belief that such things are only for the feeble minded?

Anna's curiosity was winning the tug of war going on inside her. Her feet were moving again, and before Anna realized what was happening she was walking up the steps, moving closer to the spot she was so afraid of confronting. She realized it appeared to have little to do with the stone bed or the possibility that St. Francis's energy might still linger there, but something much more alarming. If she felt the energy again then it would be hard for Anna to deny . . . what? What was it she had been denying for so long? That God exists? That Heaven is real? That she really was connected to St. Francis? Her denials were like a warm blanket that covered things too frightening for Anna to consider. If she took one more step, lay down, and felt the same energy coursing through her, it would be the end of everything she believed.

."Tell me, what you are feeling right now?"

Anna looked down and saw Padre Nicola standing just inside the door.

"What am I feeling?" she repeated, wondering how honest she should be. "I just wanted to have a final look at the spot. It's my last opportunity since I need to get walking again."

"I've lived here for so many years," the priest said to her, "and I've met so many people who come looking for something that remains of St. Francis—some kind of energy or spark. They climb those steps and they lie down, and nearly all of them feel something move inside them. But here's the thing they don't understand—it isn't St. Francis. They're feeling themselves—who they really are—though they usually deny it. It's easier to think that it's a saint who lived eight hundred years ago than something that's been resting within them the whole time. They're just finally giving it permission to come out. Something magical happens when they realize there's a Divine Spark within everyone. If the spark's given the chance to breathe it turns into a tiny flame, then into a great fire that warms everyone around them, or even changes the world. That's what happened to St. Francis, and it's happening again through everyone who comes through that door." Then he shrugged. "But what do I know? I'm just a simple friar who smiles at people when they come to visit."

Anna turned and walked down the steps till she was standing in front of Padre Nicola.

"So you don't think his energy is still here?"

"I do believe it's here, just like the energy of everyone who has come here since. You'll leave something of yourself here as well, Anna. Whenever we feel great love it anchors itself where we stand. We can go back to that place whenever we want because love transcends all boundaries. You can come here just by remembering the feeling you experienced when you lay on the stone bed yesterday."

"How did you know I felt something?" she asked.

"I could see it in your eyes," he said with a smile. "Something changed, and it's still there. I know it's confusing but it doesn't need to be. We just have to keep putting wood on the fire."

"I'm not sure I understand what you mean, Padre."

"Everyone wants to sit around a fire that's burning bright, yes? But when we neglect the fire it starts to die and before long there're only embers left. But God would never let it go out completely. Even if there's only one ember left, you can breathe oxygen onto it and it will grow and spread, ready to be fed with little twigs (because if you put on a whole log it would suffocate the tiny flame). Before long, when it's burning bright, you can put on as many logs as you want. Do you see what I mean, Anna? When people walk the Camino of Saint Francis it's like putting twigs on the fire of their soul. I think that's why so many people walk the camino, because it reignites the fire of God within them."

"But Father, I don't think I believe in God anymore. When I was a child I felt that fire, but it went out long ago."

"Like I said, it never goes out, Anna. And it doesn't matter if you believe in God or not. The important thing is that God believes in you, and there's nothing you can do to change that."

"There you are! I thought you left without me." And there was Giovanni coming around the corner with a big smile, which Anna met with one of her own, realizing with relief that he was still with her.

"We never leave one another," Padre Nicola said, "especially when we walk this camino together."

7

A Woman in Citerna

Anna followed Giovanni as they entered a dense, damp forest with tangled vegetation. They walked toward Sasso Spicco, or "jutting-out rock," which, as Giovanni explained, had been one of St. Francis's favorite places to pray. Amid the streams and waterfalls he was completely alone, one with nature and one with God.

"There are two wonderful stories about the Poverello that took place here," Giovanni said to Anna as they stood next to a huge cliff. "One is true and the other is a myth. Would you like to guess which one?"

"I guess." They began walking, Anna keeping pace with him, stretching to match her steps to his longer ones. "How can you be certain either of them is true? What if they're both myths?"

Giovanni stopped on the path and looked at her. "You have to play by the rules, Anna," he said with a wide smile. "Are you ready?"

"Go ahead," she said mockingly as they began walking again. "I'll play along."

"Good. I'll begin with the story about the two rich men from Sansepolcro who came to Francesco at Montecasale asking to be received into the order." Giovanni walked in front of Anna through a narrow part of the trail, speaking over his shoulder. "You should know that the Poverello often asked his brothers to perform illogical tasks or unusual projects to see if they were ready to live the humble life of a lesser brother. He took the men down to the garden—which we just passed, by the way—and told them to plant two rows of cabbage, one each. But there was a twist. Francesco wanted them to plant the cabbage upside down, with the leaves buried in the ground and the roots pointing up toward the sky.

"The first man did not say a word and set out immediately, planting the cabbage in the way Francesco requested.

"The other man, certain that Francesco was an imbecile, protested, pointed out that this was obviously the wrong way to plant the vegetables. Francesco smiled at him and agreed, saying, 'You are a wise and learned man. It would be best for you to return to your home and apply your wisdom where it is needed most.' The man shrugged and left, returning to Sansepolcro as he was told.

"Then Francesco turned to the first man, the one who had planted the cabbage in the manner he requested, and who was weeping. The man said sorrowfully to the Poverello, 'I am so ignorant. I thought it was the wrong way but I decided you knew best and planted them as you instructed. It's clear that I'm not ready to be one of your brothers.' Francesco threw his arms around the man and said: 'Little brother, that job had very little to do with the cabbage. This was really a lesson about obedience and humility—and you passed on both accounts. I would be honored to call you my brother.'"

Anna stopped in her tracks. "Obedience? Really? So it doesn't matter if the assignment made any sense, just that he followed orders?"

"You make it sound so negative," Giovanni said. "The lesson was about surrendering, which means giving up your ideas of what you believe needs to happen. Francesco wanted to know if they would perform a ridiculous task because they were asked to, even though they knew it was not the correct way to plant the cabbage."

"That's how cults get started," she said to him. "Everyone needs to surrender to the master or the guru. St. Francis doesn't seem any different than that."

"Here's the difference," Giovanni said. "Cult leaders today focus on getting people to surrender to them . . . to the leader. Yes? They want their disciples to turn their power over to them so they can have more control. In the case of the two men from Sansepolcro, the purpose wasn't to get them to surrender to a man, but to see if they were willing to surrender everything to God. That's always the lesson."

"This is one of those topics we're not going to agree on," Anna said to him. "Let's move on to the next story."

They began walking again and Giovanni continued. "The second story follows the first. The man who followed the bizarre instructions to plant the cabbage upside down was accepted into the order and a few years later became the guardian of the hermitage. His name was Friar Angelo. One day two famous thieves came to the door and asked Friar Angelo for some food. Well, you can imagine the outrage the brother felt. He berated the thieves and said it was terrible what they were doing, stealing from innocent people, and it was even worse that they would come to the door of humble monks and take food from their mouths. The thieves felt guilty and left empty handed. Francesco heard about this a few days later when he came to Montecasale and asked to speak with Friar Angelo alone. Francesco scolded him for acting contrary to the rules of charity and the teachings of Christ. 'Sinners are brought back to God with kindness, not harsh rebukes,' Francesco said. He told Angelo to go out and find the men, ask for their forgiveness, then bring them back to the monastery where they would be welcomed as family. Of course Angelo followed the instructions and when he found the thieves threw himself on the ground and begged for their forgiveness. He brought them back to Montecasale and they were treated like kings at a feast."

There was a long pause as Giovanni looked at Anna. "Is that it?" she asked him.

"Actually, it isn't. Those two thieves spent the rest of their lives in the hermitage. That's how moved they were by the charity that was shown to them." They stopped beneath a large fir. "Now that you've heard both stories, tell me which one you think a myth."

"They both sound like fiction to me," she said, taking off her pack and balancing her walking stick against the tree. "That's the thing about stories that happened eight hundred years ago—it's impossible to separate the fact from the fantasy. My mother used to tell me stories about St. Francis and St. Clare that I believed when I was young, but when I got older I decided that most of them were too fantastic to be true."

"Like what?" Giovanni asked her.

"Like birds listening to him preach because the people of a town refused to listen," She said. "Or how about when he was in France and he wanted to send a sack of bread to his brothers in Folloni—I believe that's where it was."

"I know the story," Giovanni said. "It was the friary in Folloni."

"Well, as you know, since St. Francis lived in thirteenth century France he couldn't send the package by courier, so he summoned an angel to carry the bag to the friary. The brothers heard a knock on the door, though the brother that answered found only a bag filled with bread to feed the starving monks. My mother used to tell me that story, and I thought it was amazing. I totally believed it. What makes that story different from the two you told?"

"You may be interested to know that scientific studies have been done on pieces of cloth that came from the bag you described," Giovanni said to her. "Obviously there's no way to prove that an angel brought it there, but they did prove that the dates line up and that bread had been in the sack. But I can't tell you anything more about the other two stories until you make your guess."

"Nothing about St. Francis preaching to the birds, eh?"

"Not until you answer my question. Which of the stories is a myth?"

Anna looked up at the trees and considered her options. Planting the cabbage upside down seemed like a classic romantic tale that was rarely based on fact, and though the story of the thieves asking for food had a better ring, the ending seemed a bit far-fetched.

"I'm going to say that the story of the thieves is the myth," she said to him. "Most stories of St. Francis make him seem a bit crazy, so I'm going with that one. I can't believe that the two thieves would move in and become monks just because they were fed a good meal."

"So you think the story of planting the cabbage upside down is true?"

"Not really," Anna answered, "but if you insist on me choosing only one I have to go with the thieves."

Giovanni smiled at her and said: "I lied to you, Anna. When I told you that one of the stories is a myth I was not being honest. Neither are myths—both are completely true."

"I don't believe you—and why would you do that to me?" she scolded. "How can you know any of this with such certainty? Just because you read the stories in a book doesn't mean either of them is true."

"It's true that I've read the stories in books," Giovanni answered, "but that's not how I know they're true."

He started to walk again, and Anna quickly grabbed her stick and threw her backpack over her shoulder. "So, how, then?" she asked, but as she spoke something unusual began to happen. The forest, which had been completely quiet until that moment, was suddenly alive with activity. Birds seemed to come from nowhere, singing together like a great choir. Anna looked up into the trees and saw birds of different sizes and colors flying back and forth, or sitting high atop the branches. The sound continued for at least a minute and then, as suddenly as they began, the birds lit toward the sky and were gone. The forest was quiet again.

She stood there watching Giovanni's back for some time before continuing to follow him.

T

After visiting Sasso Spicco, Anna and Giovanni walked on to Sansepolcro, a city that impressed Anna so deeply she wanted to stay the night and explore during what was left of the afternoon. Thanks to the reign of the Medici family, its soaring architecture was so grand it reminded her of Florence, though much smaller. However, Giovanni, suggested they keep walking to the town of Citerna, which was another eight miles. He had a feeling, he told Anna. Something good was going to happen there.

Having learned to trust Giovanni's hunches, Anna agreed. They enjoyed a pleasant walk through the lowlands with soft climbs and gentle descents through the hills of the Valtiberina, leading away from the rich and varied blessings of Tuscany to the border of Umbria. They passed a group of houses and entered the tiny village of Bastia, in the Perugia province, and stepped into Umbria for the first time. Anna was back in her home region for the first time in decades, and she could feel her approach to Assisi gaining momentum. After leaving Bastia they alternated between asphalt roads and dirt paths, passing the Torre del Guando agritourism farm, completing the entire lowland stretch of the Tiber upper valley. Before long they began climbing again and within a short distance found themselves at the gates of Citerna.

"Did you know that Citerna was named one of the prettiest villages in Italy?" Giovanni asked Anna as they walked through the Porta Fiorentina gate. They were walking toward the Piazza Scipioni because Giovanni was convinced something important would happen there.

"It reminds me a bit of Assisi," Anna said.

"Yes, but Assisi before so many tourists. Citerna has such a sweet energy that hasn't changed in hundreds of years."

"I'm putting a lot of trust in you today," Anna said. "I know you think something important is going to happen here, but part of me wonders if you've gone a bit crazy."

"I've learned to trust my intuition," Giovanni told her. "In my experience, there's a quiet voice inside each of us and if we listen to its guidance our lives find a natural balance. Other voices, like the ego, may be much louder, but the subtle voice of the soul always knows more. The ego is like a two-year-old child, always crying and trying to get its way, but when the child lies down for sleep, that's when the soul can sing."

They arrived in the Piazza Scipioni. Anna dropped her backpack on the ground and walked to the edge where she could see the valley that stretched out beneath them. As she massaged her aching legs, she watched the clouds roll in and the sun cast shadows on the earth below, giving the impression the countryside had come to life. A small cafe was alive with activity behind her, and on the other side of the piazza she noticed a sharp incline that led to a large church. Beside the incline, an ancient clock tower rang. She looked at Giovanni who seemed amused at her reaction.

"It's so beautiful," she said to him. "I'm glad you suggested it."

"The church is dedicated to the Poverello," he said, "and then there's the Camminamento Medievale—the medieval walkway—with covered passageways that date back to the Middle Ages."

"I would like to see it, but not quite yet. I want to stand here and look around a bit longer."

"Actually," Giovanni said with some urgency, "I think we should go now. Follow me."

Giovanni led her through town, and within seconds they had arrived at a passageway with stunning arched openings that gave view to the valley, and the wooden timbers supporting the roof of the ancient path—surely a favorite place for romantic walks and late-night strolls.

Giovanni walked as if late for an appointment, and Anna followed, wondering if his latest starry-eyed vision would again end in some mysterious event. She could be sitting alone at the cafe enjoying a glass of wine looking over the lowlands as the sun began to set, but this at least had the taste of adventure, so she was happy to go along.

Two or three people passed them as they walked but Giovanni did not seem to notice. He had yet to reveal where he was taking her or whom they were going to meet but seemed to walk with deliberate aim. Then Anna spotted a young woman, perhaps a few years younger than Giovanni, standing in front of one of the arched openings looking out over the valley, her long blonde hair loose and what appeared to be a small blanket wrapped around her shoulders. Giovanni stopped as if he had found his mark. He turned to Anna and said, "It's best that you wait here. I need to have a conversation that might be uncomfortable without privacy."

Then he walked toward the woman, and Anna waited where she stood. She imagined that the woman was a former girlfriend or perhaps one Giovanni was pursuing. The thought made her feel uncomfortable and a bit agitated. This is why he insisted on rushing to the town, to initiate an encounter that had nothing to do with her? She considered leaving and going back to the piazza, but there was something about Giovanni's manner that made her wait. She watched as he approached the woman, and when she turned and saw him she seemed shocked by his sudden appearance. He stood close and whispered something in a low voice, as if sharing something private and discreet. Shock turned to tears, and the woman hid her face in her hands. Giovanni stepped closer and wrapped his arms around her, and they stood there, embracing, for a long time. They talked for several minutes, until Anna noticed the tears had been replaced with wide smile. Then Giovanni led her back to the place where Anna stood waiting. "Anna, I want you to meet someone," he said. "This is Sofia. Sofia, this is my friend Anna. We have been walking together toward Assisi."

"It's very nice to meet you," Sofia said to Anna, kissing both cheeks.

Anna wasn't sure what to say. She felt like an intruder and wished she wasn't there to interfere with whatever was taking place between them. "Likewise, but I shouldn't intrude," she said looking straight at Giovanni. "It's best that you have time alone to catch up or . . . ." Anna felt awkward saying anything. She began to turn and walk away when Sofia said, "But this is the first time we've met. I came here to be alone, then I looked up and he was there."

"Then maybe the two of you need to stay together for awhile," Anna said. "I'm just in the way."

"But Anna, you're the reason I went to speak to Sofia," Giovanni said.

Anna was surprised. She had no idea why Giovanni felt such a strong urge to rush from Sansepolcro to Citerna to find a woman neither of them had met before.

"What do I have to do with any of this?" she asked him.

"Come with me," Giovanni said, walking down the narrow passageway till they were back on the street heading toward the piazza. They walked in silence, though now and then Anna looked over her shoulder at Sofia who was walking in the rear. She picked up her pace to walk beside Giovanni.

"What's happening?" Anna asked. "If this is someone you're inter-ested in—leave me out of it. I'll just find a hotel, and we can meet in the morning if that's what you want."

Giovanni looked at her and smiled. "Everything will make sense in a few minutes, Anna. Just trust me."

When they reached the piazza, Giovanni motioned for them to sit down on one of the benches looking out over the valley. It was dark, except for the flickering lights from the houses and farms and a few cars and trucks moving along the highway, which stretched from one side of the landscape to the other. Giovanni stationed himself on one end of the bench and asked the two women to sit together with Anna in the middle. Sofia looked down at the cement as if she had just gone through a terrible ordeal, and Anna looked at Giovanni to show she was losing patience.

"Sofia knows that you're from America but that you were raised here in Italy," Giovanni said. "I explained to her that you were forced to leave and this is the first time you've been back since you were young, not much younger than Sofia is now."

"What does that have to do with anything?" Anna said. Then she turned to Sofia. "You seem like a very nice girl, but I'm a bit lost right now. I thought maybe Giovanni liked you and wanted to spend time with you, but now I don't have any idea what's happening."

"I wanted the two of you to meet because you share something very unique," Giovanni continued. "There is something happening to Sofia that you will understand, Anna."

"The only thing I understand is you've lost your mind," Anna said. "Why did you pull this poor girl up here only. . . ."

"I'm pregnant," Sofia interrupted. "I don't know how he knew, but it's true. I went to the Camminamento Medievale to be alone and think. I just found out a few days ago and haven't told my family yet. They're going to be so upset, and I don't know what they'll do."

Anna looked at Giovanni who was gazing at Sofia with the softest eyes she had ever seen. She wanted to lash out at him, to tell him how inappropriate it was to intrude on this delicate situation. But how had he known? That Sofia would be standing in the walkway, at that very moment, and that he had to get there before. . . .

"Why were you standing there when we came by?" Anna asked Sofia.

"I don't know," she said as tears began to roll down her cheeks. "I don't know why I was there. I was so confused, I thought maybe it was best. . . ."

She was crying too hard to speak and Anna wrapped her arms around the girl, holding her close to muffle her sobs. Giovanni sat motionless.

"I understand," Anna said to her. "I once considered the same thing." Sofia looked up at her and wiped away her tears.

"What do you mean?" she asked. "You thought about jumping?"

"I did. When I was seventeen I met a boy and things got out of hand. I was pregnant, and my family was terrified of what would happen if people in Assisi found out. They shipped me off to America, but on the way I thought about taking my life. The only thing that stopped me was the child I felt growing within my body. I knew I couldn't do that to her. Not long after I arrived in the US I met a man and fell in love. He didn't care that I was pregnant and we built a life together."

"So you were happy you decided to live?" Sofia asked.

"Of course I was, silly girl. It was the best decision I ever made, and it will be the same for you. There is a life growing inside you, and it doesn't matter what anyone thinks about it. It doesn't matter how it happened or why, only that you're here now and you need to carry on, for your child's sake."

Sofia threw her arms around Anna again and held her tight.

"You are the answer to a prayer," she said.

Anna glanced at Giovanni and smiled. It didn't matter how he knew. Nothing mattered but the young girl from Citerna. She wondered why it was so easy to talk to Sofia about the subject she had kept from her own daughter for so long. She felt some of her own shame disappear, because she was helping someone—helping a young girl no different from herself when she was young.

Later that night Anna felt an intense desire to speak with Kay. Her time with Sofia had sparked the trauma as well as the joy she had felt raising her only child. At one point she had regretted her decision not to have other children, but since Penny was born even that had changed. What would her life have been like if she hadn't become pregnant and left Italy? Her daughter and granddaughter were her greatest gifts, and she couldn't imagine life without them. She was sure Sofia could have the same experience when she was older. Anna hoped she'd experience the same love Anna had found through her own children and grandchildren.

"Mom, it's so good to hear from you," Kay said when she picked up the phone. "How are you?"

"I fell and sprained my wrist on day two and my legs are killing me," Anna said. "Other than that, I'm great."

"I've been so worried but didn't want to call. I was afraid I'd interrupt something. It was really tough, though."

"I met someone, Kay," Anna said to her, quickly realizing how her daughter would interpret the remark.

"You met someone? A man? You're kidding me."

"Not like that. Yes, he's a man but he's younger than you are. He's my walking companion. Giovanni. A young Italian. I'll tell you the truth, honey, I don't think I could do it without him"

"So you go off to Italy and meet a younger man," Kay joked, "and all you have to say is that he's your walking companion."

"Oh, stop it. I didn't come here to find a partner, I came here to . . . let things go. That's the best way to explain it."

"Finally," Kay said. "I'm finally hearing why you're on this crazy journey. You're letting things go . . . and I won't press you for more. I'm sure you'll tell me more when you can."

"I will . . . I promise. But there is something I want to tell you right now." She took a deep breath. "I love you, honey. More than you'll ever know. And you made me the happiest woman in the world when you brought Penny into the world."

There was a long silence on the other end of the phone, and Anna wondered if the lines were still connected.

"Kay, are you there?" she asked.

"Yes, Mom, I'm still here. I'm just touched, that's all. You know how much we love you . . . in fact, there's someone here who wants to say something." There was a pause and a rustling, then Anna heard the familiar voice on the other end of the phone.

"Nana. . . . I miss you," Penny said.

"And grandma misses you so much, Penny. Are you being a good girl for your mom?"

"Yes."

"That's good, sweetheart. You just listen to her, and tell her you can call me whenever you want. And I'll be home before you know it. I love you, Penny."

"Goodbye, Nana. I love you too."

"Okay, Mom, I'm going to let you go now," Kay said when she came back on the line. "I know it's late there and you need your rest. And thank you for what you said. It means a lot to me."

"Okay, honey. I'll call you in a couple more days."

"And watch out for that Giovanni guy. You know how Italian men are."

"Have a wonderful day, honey."

She hung up the phone and took a deep breath. "I'm a lucky woman," she thought, and something else, "I feel younger." She wasn't the old lady who had started the camino but the vibrant fifty-something woman she actually was. Why had she surrendered to time so easily?

When her husband died, Anna had wondered whether there was enough left to live for. But then Penny was born, and she had decided she would live for her. She stretched out on the bed and took another deep breath. For the first time in years Anna felt like a new chapter of her life had just begun.

8

PERFECT JOY

Giovanni slept under the stars that night, and Anna took a room in a small hostel named Madre Teresa, a short walk from where they would begin the next day's journey. She knew Giovanni was close by, but the distance still made her uneasy. Anna lay in her bed wondering if she was becoming emotionally dependent on her camino partner. Had Kay's joke triggered the feeling? Or had his help captured her in ways she wouldn't have expected when they first met at La Verna? And then there were the "events" that were beginning to occur with greater frequency, such as the bird choir when they left the Hermitage of Montecasale, or the way he found Sofia on the Camminamento Medievale. Anna could explain them easily enough—the appearance of the birds being a bizarre coincidence and finding Sofia a stroke of luck. But her suspicious nature was softening.

"What am I going to do with this kid?" she thought to herself as she drifted off to sleep.

The next morning Giovanni was waiting for her in the lobby.

"Good morning, Anna," he said, holding up a cup of fresh coffee. "I think you like a café latte, yes?"

"That's correct," she said, putting down the guidebook and taking the cup, "and God bless you for this."

"A blessing so early? You're changing before my eyes, Anna."

"Anyone who gives me coffee in the morning gets a standard blessing," Anna said. "It's general policy."

"Today we're going to have a short walk," Giovanni said, picking up the guidebook from where she had set it. "And you can put this away. You don't need it as long as you're with me."

Anna took the guidebook back and stowed it in her backpack, which she then slung over her shoulder.

"Then lead the way, Brother Guide. My life is in your hands."

And with that they were on their way to Città di Castello, a large town on the left bank of the Tiber River. They passed a small chapel, then descended a hill till they reached an asphalt road that led into Monterchi, then the lane that led to Patrignone. They began climbing again, along a path that curved to the left, until they reached a cart track that entered a chestnut wood. They continued to climb until reaching the crest of the hill where a magnificent view of the valley spread out below them.

Anna, needing a rest, watched the stunning vista as clouds gathered, but the wind insisted they continue. They passed through the little village of Celle standing proud at the top of the hill, then through Caldese, where they began the descent and joined another asphalt road.

"I want to show you something," Giovanni said. They came around a bend in the road and Anna saw a great herd of buffalo. "They're different from the buffalo you have in the US, but you must try the mozzarella at the farm. It's very famous here in Italy. This herd is much smaller than those you'll find in Campania in the South."

They arrived at the farm and Giovanni introduced Anna to the farmer, who sat them down at a table and served them a beautiful salad with cheese made from his herd. After lunch, they left the farm and returned to the trail, which soon went up a gentle hill and down again to the town of Lerchi. In the distance they could see their destination—Città di Castello. The descent turned steep till they reached the village of San Lorenzo. They continued for five miles through a vineyard that sloped gently downward until they came to another asphalt road.

"There's another hermitage I'd like to show you," Giovanni said to Anna. "This one is very special."

"They all seem special to you," she observed, her walking stick thumping against the dry earth. "They seem to be everywhere."

"Many of them have stories of when the Poverello visited," he continued. "This one, Eremo di Buon Riposo, is unusual and quite beautiful, though we'll need permission to enter. It's made from ancient caves that Francesco loved to visit when he was on his way to and from La Verna. I have the feeling we need to stop."

"You're the guide," Anna said, paying more attention to the pain in her feet than what he was saying. She was beginning to think once you've seen one hermitage you've seen them all, but on this day she didn't feel like arguing.

When they reached the small lane that led to the entrance, Giovanni said, "You should wait here. I'll find someone who can welcome us."

"How much further is Città di Castello?" Anna asked. "My feet are really starting to hurt. I'm not sure I can make it all the way."

Giovanni motioned for her to sit down on a large boulder at the side of the path and asked her to take off her shoes and socks. When she did, Anna was alarmed to see that a large blister had formed on each of her big toes.

"How bad are they?" she asked him.

"Not too bad, but you shouldn't walk any further till we get them bandaged. Wait here and I'll see if I can get some help." Giovanni walked toward the hermitage, leaving Anna sitting on the boulder. She looked again at the blisters and winced. The pain was beginning to mount, and she knew she was done walking for the day. She needed a warm place to rest her aching muscles and blistered feet, though she didn't relish the thought of another hermitage. Then Anna heard the sound of someone singing and walking in her direction. She turned and saw a plump young friar looking up toward the sky singing in Italian. Anna realized she had to say something or risk the man tripping right over her.

"Watch your step," she said quietly, hoping she didn't startle him. He looked down and jumped back, surprised to see anyone sitting on the rock at the entrance to his home.

"What are you doing here?" he asked. "You scared me nearly to death."

"I'm waiting for my friend," Anna told him, "and if you were watching where you were going you would have seen me."

The friar didn't like this response. He looked down on Anna as if looking at someone of a lower caste.

"You shouldn't be here at all," he said. "Don't you know where you are? This is a Franciscan friary. Women aren't allowed without permission. You should leave right away."

Anna stood up to face the man and realized she was at least three inches taller than he. He stepped back when he saw the determination on her face but maintained his arrogance.

"First of all, as you can see I'm having trouble," she said pointing down at her uncovered feet. "I have blisters. And, secondly, I told you I'm waiting for someone."

The friar huffed, taking a step closer to Anna as he said, "Who do you think you're talking to? I'm a priest. You don't have any say over who we allow in the hermitage, even if you do have blisters. Now I'm not going to say it again—please be on your way."

Anna was so angry she didn't hear Giovanni approaching. When he realized what was happening he immediately stepped between them.

"Greetings, Brother. My name is Giovanni. Is everything okay?"

"I'm a priest not a brother. And as I was just telling your friend, you're not welcome here. It doesn't matter to me if her feet hurt a little. You're the ones who wanted to walk the camino, not me. I'm tired of people coming to our hermitage with their rucksacks and walking sticks. There's nothing special about walking all day and then getting drunk at night."

"But Father, we're walking in imitation of the Poverello who was walking in imitation of Christ. Shouldn't a friar like you welcome such pilgrims?" By this time the priest's attitude was fully formed. He walked to the gate that led to the hermitage and closed it so that Anna and Giovanni couldn't come any closer.

"Don't tell me who I should or shouldn't welcome. I've dedicated my life to living like St. Francis, and all you're doing is walking from town to town, thinking you're special. Well, you're not. Now be on your way, or I'll call the police."

Giovanni stepped closer to the gate and put his hands on the metal bar. The friar stepped back, as if afraid of being struck.

"Dear Father," Giovanni said, "As you see my friend cannot walk any further today. It would be dangerous for her to continue. Is there anywhere we can rest for the night and then leave for Città di Castello in the morning?"

The friar's features rolled together like a wet rag being wrung out. He pointed toward a small, dilapidated shed a hundred feet down the driveway. "You can sleep in the shed for the night, but I'm going to come and check in the morning and you had better be gone."

Anna stepped forward, ready for a final battle, but Giovanni took hold of her arm and held her back.

"That would be fine, Father. We know the way to Assisi is often hard. We are very grateful for your kindness."

Having won the battle, the friar turned and left.

"Why did you let him off so easy?" Anna asked.

"He actually gave us a great gift," Giovanni told her, "to remain humble in the face of maltreatment."

"There you go again," she said to him. "I'm not going to sleep on the floor of some broken-down shed when they probably have rooms in the hermitage we could use."

"It doesn't seem we have an option. We need to get your blisters bandaged before we do anything."

"And how are we going to do that?" she asked.

"Don't worry about that for a second," Giovanni said over his shoulder as he started toward the shed. "It's already in motion."

Two hours later Giovanni and Anna sat on opposite sides of the shed, which had by then grown damp and cold. She wanted a room with a bed where she could get a good night's sleep. Instead they were huddled in a tiny scrap of a building with no water, food, or bathroom. Giovanni seemed to take it all in stride, as if he knew something she didn't. And what did "It's already in motion" mean? It sounded like wishful thinking.

They heard a gentle knock on the flimsy door. They stood and Giovanni opened it to find an elderly friar holding several blankets, two pillows, and a canvas bag. He came in and looked around, then set the load on a decrepit-looking bench.

"Dear children," the priest said, "I have come to ask for your forgiveness." There were two chairs in the shed, and Giovanni motioned for him to sit in one and Anna in the other. Giovanni pulled up a stout piece of wood that was resting in the corner and sat down with them.

"Father, there's no need for forgiveness," Giovanni said.

Anna protested, "Perhaps not for him but the other priest was—"

"I know," the friar said quickly, "he was terribly unwelcoming. Father Juniper is a young friar, and there is so much for him to learn about Franciscan hospitality. My name is Father Anthony. I'm the guardian of this community. I came out to see you myself and bring you these so you'll be warm and well fed."

"It is very kind of you, Father Anthony," Giovanni said to him. "We're walking the Camino of St. Francis. We are happy for this little castle."

Anna looked at Giovanni, not sure if she should speak her mind. She was genuinely moved by this priest's actions. It certainly took the sting away from having to sleep in the hovel.

"I'm more upset than my young friend," Anna said, "but I'm grateful you've come to help."

"I hear one of you is suffering from blisters," Father Anthony said as he reached into the pockets of his habit and produced ointment, a roll of gauze, and tape. "When I first came here we had pilgrims coming through the hermitage almost every day, and I was in charge of serving them. I can't tell you how many blisters I've nursed. Which one of you needs the help?"

Anna pulled up her pant leg and showed the bottom of her feet. Friar Anthony shifted his chair so he could lift her foot into his lap and then went to work.

"There is a story about St. Francis I've always loved," he continued. "One winter's day, as Saint Francis was traveling with Brother Leo from Perugia to Saint Mary of the Angels to see the brothers, he said: 'Brother Leo, if God were to make of the friars' great examples of holiness and humility, for me this would not be perfect joy.' A little while later Francis turned to Leo again and said: 'Brother Leo, if the friars were able to make the lame walk, give sight to the blind, heal the deaf, give speech back to the dumb, and even raise the dead, I tell you, this would not be perfect joy.' By this time Leo knew Francis was building up to something important, so he wasn't surprised when Francis turned to him yet again and said, 'Brother Leo, if the friars knew all the languages in the world, were well-versed in science, could explain the loftiest scriptures, and had the gift of prophesy, still for me this would not be perfect joy.' Well, this went on and on until Leo couldn't stand it any longer and he asked St. Francis to please tell him what perfect joy would be. Francis smiled at him and said: 'If, when we arrive at St. Mary of the Angels, drenched with rain, covered in mud, and exhausted from hunger, if we knocked on the convent gate and the guard asked who we were and we said, 'We are your brothers,' and the guard angrily said, 'You're both imposters and have no place here,' then shut the door in our faces leaving us in the cold and the rain . . . if we should bear this injustice with humility and grace, oh, Brother Leo, to me this would be perfect joy.'"

"I love that story," Giovanni said.

"I don't understand it at all," Anna answered as Father Anthony began wrapping her left foot.

"It's simple," he said. "Nothing was more important to St. Francis than being happy regardless of what happened around him. If he came to the door of his own home after being insulted and pushed away, and was able to still maintain that joy, then he would count it as perfect. It's easy to be happy when things are going your way, but when you find joy in a situation where you're being abused and are grateful for even that, that is the greatest joy he could imagine."

Father Anthony stayed with them for several hours. The cold night turned warmer and brighter as they talked and shared. Anna noticed the honor Giovanni showed the priest, and she realized that this man was a true Franciscan. Then she remembered Sister Celeste, the nun at La Verna who gave her the walking stick that had proven so valuable. She was also a true Franciscan. She offered up a silent prayer for the nun, just as she had promised.

"Don't look now, Anna," she said to herself, "but you're starting to get soft on all these priests and nuns."

Then she curled up beneath her blanket and closed her eyes, a feeling of gratitude filling her heart as she drifted off to sleep.

9

DEFINITION OF A MIRACLE

"I haven't smoked a cigarette in five days," Anna said to Giovanni when they awoke the next morning. Giovanni was already putting his few belongings into his tiny bag.

"I hadn't noticed," he said with a wry smile, which meant he had noticed indeed.

"I really believe you're weaving some kind of spell over me. I've been a smoker most of my life and I've tried quitting at least five times, probably more. I even have two unopened packs in my bag so I wouldn't run out. No desire at all. And my legs aren't aching like before either."

"And why are you surprised that it would happen when you walk the camino?" He asked.

"Like I said, I've never been able to stop before now. Suddenly it occurs to me that I don't even want one. That's quite a miracle."

Giovanni finished his packing and tightened the cord that secured the bag.

"And here I didn't think you believed in miracles," he said to her.

"Who said I do," Anna said with a wink as she threw her pack over her shoulder, then stepped out the small door to begin another day's walk.

They crossed the Tiber River an hour later, after descending a long, gentle hill along a winding dirt road. They approached Città di Castello and as soon as they entered the town, Giovanni turned to Anna, "There's

85

a very interesting story about the Poverello that took place in this town," he said. "But first I have to ask you what may seem like a strange question."

"Most of your questions are strange," she said to him, "so go ahead."

"Do you believe in possession?"

"What kind of a question is that?" Anna asked surprised. "I saw *The Exorcist* and thought it was ridiculous."

"That was a movie," he said to her. "I'm talking real world. Do you think it's possible for an evil spirit to enter a person's body?"

Anna was walking in front of Giovanni as he asked this. She spun around, wondering if he was joking or just trying to rouse an energetic response. "Of course I don't believe in possession. Wouldn't a person need to believe in God before they believe in possession?"

"I was hoping you were past that by now," he said.

"Past not believing in God?" she said thoughtfully. "You've nudged me closer to the fence but I'm not there yet."

"Well, let me tell you the story and we'll see if it brings you any closer," he said as they started walking again. "It happened right here in Città di Castello. Francesco was staying nearby and the townspeople brought him a woman in the throes of a demonic attack. Apparently, she had been possessed for a long time, and no one knew what to do. So they decided to ask Francesco when they heard he was coming their way. Francesco was suspicious, thinking perhaps the woman was pretending to be possessed to gain attention. So instead of going outside he sent one of his brothers who was there with him. 'But the woman will believe I am you,' the brother said to him. 'If she does, then we'll know she is not possessed,' Francesco answered. So straight away the friar went outside and stood before the woman without saying a word. 'Why do you send me a lamb when you have a lion inside?' the woman demanded. Francesco realized that the story was true—the woman was indeed possessed. He went outside and sat down on the ground in front of her, at which the woman began wailing and writhing. Francesco waited till she finally became still. 'In virtue of obedience I bid you leave this poor woman,' he said, and seconds later the woman's face softened and she began to cry, overjoyed that she was finally released."

Anna looked at Giovanni incredulously. "Do you really believe that story?" she asked, unable to prevent a roll of her eyes.

"So, you believe it's fiction?"

"Of course. There are a hundred possible explanations for what happened—if it ever happened at all."

"Are there any you can think of?" Giovanni asked.

Anna thought for a moment and said, "Saint Francis was a famous guy at that point, right?"

"He was, but not in the way we think of fame now."

"Obviously there was no internet nor were there any photographs, but it's possible she saw him or heard someone describe how he looks. Maybe the other friar was a tall man, and she knew Francesco was short. The fact that she realized it wasn't him isn't proof she was possessed."

"Okay," Giovanni said, never losing his smile, "let's say you're right. Let's say she wasn't actually possessed by a demon but thought she was. Isn't it possible that Francesco gave her an even greater gift?"

"What do you mean?"

"He helped restore peace to her mind. No one can prove whether she was or wasn't possessed, but I do believe the basis of the story. It was written by Francesco's first biographer Thomas of Celano, not long after Francesco left the world. Perhaps the woman had a mental disorder and he cured her. Wouldn't that still be a miracle?"

"Autosuggestion," Anna darted back. "Just because someone is hypnotized into believing they're healed from a malady that didn't even exist doesn't make it a miracle."

"I guess it depends on your definition of a miracle," Giovanni said.

"A miracle is something that couldn't have happened in any other way," she said. "It can't be explained through science or normal physics."

"Of course you're right," he answered. "But here's something to consider. There was a famous friar named Padre Pio who lived in a monastery called San Giovanni Rotondo. Padre Pio had predicted that their village would not be bombed by the allied forces during World War II. This was quite a prediction, since most towns around them had been bombed or destroyed. Near the city of Bari there was an allied base with pilots of various nationalities stationed. They determined there was a cache of Nazi weapons in San Giovanni Rotondo and were intent on destroying it. Many missions were sent out to complete the task and all returned saying the same thing: When they approached the target area they saw a monk floating in the sky, his hands raised and motioning for them to go away. Not one bomb fell on the town. An American commander at the base decided to lead a bombing raid himself. Sure enough, when he returned to the base he was beside himself with terror and told a familiar story: As they neared the drop point they saw the same flying monk telling them to go back. Before they could react, the bombs released on their own and fell in a nearby forest. After the war, the commander and a few of his pilots went to visit San Giovanni Rotondo and as soon as they arrived they met Padre Pio and recognized him as the flying monk.

"So, Anna, would that qualify as a miracle in your mind?"

"If I believed it, it would."

"You don't believe it happened?"

"It's just too incredible. A flying monk holding back a squadron of bombers?"

"When you get a chance, go online and look up a man named Bernardo Rosini. He was the base's commanding Italian general, and known to have a spotless reputation. He was the one who reported these events and said that it happened dozens of times. The only remaining question, dear Anna: will you trust him?"

Anna didn't know what to say. If the story was true, and she had no reason to doubt Giovanni's word, then it was a definite threat to her current mindset. Fortunately, the story was beyond ridiculous—more like a children's fairy tale than military history. But if it was true. . . .

"If what you say is accurate, then I would have to admit it was a miracle and would definitely alter my vision of the world. But trust me—I'll be doing some research of my own."

"I expect nothing less. But now I have a different question. It's easy to hear a story like that and admit the existence of a higher power, but what about the small ordinary miracles that happen every day?"

"Like a kind friar showing up at the last minute and bandaging my blisters?"

"Exactly," Giovanni said. "In fact, I want you to do something for me."

He had Anna sit down on a fallen log and asked her to take off her shoes.

"Unwrap the bandages the friar used to protect the blisters," he said to her.

"But I'll never be able to get them on again."

"You won't need to," Giovanni answered.

Anna did as Giovanni asked and unwrapped the bandages on her left foot. What she saw confounded her, so she quickly did the same with her right foot.

"That's impossible," she said in a quiet voice. "Last night they were terrible. Now. . . ."

"Now they're healed. You could say that he did an excellent job and leave it at that, but you and I both know that blisters don't heal that quickly. Now put your socks and shoes back on and let's get going."

Giovanni started walking while Anna sat there for a long moment, completely amazed.

10

No One a Stranger

The two companions passed through the town of Città di Castello, and after finding the path that cuts parallel to the Soara stream, they walked toward Pieve de' Saddi with its stunning views of the Umbrian valley. Giovanni seemed to know the trails like the back of his hand. Anna never once glanced at the guidebook, secure at the bottom of her pack.

"I want to reach Candeggio before it gets too late," Giovanni said. "I have friends who run a hostel and are true camino patrons. We'll spend the night with them."

"If you want to go all the way to Pietralunga I'm sure I could make it," Anna informed him. "My feet feel amazing."

Giovanni didn't answer but his smile never faded. Anna noticed and thought how lucky she was to have such a guide. She also wondered why so many strange things seemed to happen around him. Were they the small miracles he spoke of or just coincidences that could be easily explained? Anna felt her mind rebel but her soul seemed to have a different response. For the first time in many years she decided to listen to the deeper impulse moving within her.

They arrived at Che Passo hostel by midafternoon, and as they walked through the gate Anna heard a loud voice come from inside.

"Giovanni, it's you!"

"Roberto," Giovanni yelled, then ran to the front door where a young man stood waiting. As they hugged, a beautiful woman came out of the door to greet him.

"Look who decided to come back to us Michela," Roberto said to the woman as she greeted Giovanni with a kiss to each cheek, "like the Prodigal Son returning to his father." Francesco wrapped his arms around Michela as Roberto noticed Anna. "And it looks like you've brought someone with you again. You never walk the camino alone, do you Giovanni?"

"Never," he said. "This is my friend Anna. She's American but really an Italian native. And she doesn't believe anything about miracles or God or angels, so be gentle with her."

"What?" Michela said and she walked over to Anna. "How is that possible when you're walking to Assisi with this guy? It's all he talks about."

"That's not true," Giovanni said, "but sometimes I do get carried away."

"I've learned how to distract him," Anna joked with a warm smile. Michela wrapped her arms around Anna in a welcoming hug.

"Well, we look forward to hearing about these distractions. Welcome to our home," Michela said as she took Anna's arm. "There are only three other pilgrims here tonight so there's plenty of room."

Later Anna was sitting at the kitchen table with Michela peeling potatoes for the evening meal. Anna was impressed by the peace she felt sitting next to this young woman and how easy it was for her to welcome strangers from around the world into her home.

"No one is really a stranger," she explained to Anna, "especially when they're walking the camino. That's the reason Roberto and I opened this house—to welcome our family. We actually walked the Camino de Santiago in Spain on our honeymoon. You meet so many people, and there's something that binds you together. And now here we are welcoming people who are on their way to Assisi. By the time they get here they're so close they can almost taste it. It's very exciting for us."

"I'm doing my best to keep Assisi out of my mind," Anna said to her.

"Why is that? Why would you be walking the camino if you aren't excited to see Assisi?"

"I was raised there. I left when I was seventeen and haven't been back. And now I'm walking back, like walking into town after forty years is perfectly normal."

"There's no family for you there?" Michela asked.

"The only real family I have is back in Oregon," Anna said in a dark tone. "As for Assisi, we'll have to wait and see."

"What do you mean? You haven't contacted anyone and told them you're coming?"

"There's really no need." Then she took out the wrinkled piece of paper she had been carrying the entire journey. "See this slip of paper? Renaldo B. stands for Renaldo Bernardone. My father."

"Bernardone? Like St. Francis?" Michela said in shock.

"Yes. My maiden name. He used to say that we're distant relatives but I never believed it." Anna shrugged her shoulders. "But who knows."

"And that's who you're going to see?"

It was the first time Anna spoke aloud about her desire to see her father. In the back of her mind she didn't expect him to be there at all. And if he was, there was no way of knowing how he would respond to seeing an adult woman show up claiming to be the daughter he forced away when she was only a girl.

"I haven't been able to speak about it till now," Anna told her. "My daughter doesn't even know. And please, don't say anything to Giovanni. I don't want him bothered by any of that."

"Why do you think Giovanni wouldn't understand?" Michela asked. "I've known him for years and I've never known him to respond with anything but love."

"Speaking of Giovanni, can you tell me what you know about him? Does he always show up guiding lost little puppies like me?"

"Actually, yes," she said. "He shows up here three or four times a year, and he's never alone. He has a special way of connecting with people, and as far as I can tell he always arrives with someone who needs help in some way."

"What about women?" Anna asked her. "He's a very attractive young man. Does he ever come with a girlfriend?"

"You know, I was just thinking about that earlier today. I've never seen him with or even heard him talk about a romantic partner. It's a little strange when you think about it. A few pilgrims over the years became seriously infatuated with him, but he never seems to notice."

As Anna continued peeling the potatoes she wondered if things could turn any more bizarre. Even his close friends knew very little about Giovanni. For the first time she felt a strange energy creeping up on her that felt like a weight holding her in place. Who was this charming man who showed up in her life when she needed him most—as if out of thin air? And when she considered the astonishing events that had taken place since they began walking together, the question grew even more mysterious.

An hour later, the three other pilgrims gathered around the table enjoying the simple meal and sharing stories about their journey to Assisi. Anna said very little, speaking only when a direct question was asked of her. She watched Giovanni interact comfortably with the other pilgrims as if they were close friends, but she couldn't shake the feeling that he was hiding something from her. There were so many unanswered questions and mysteries, like how he knew Sofia would need him at such a critical moment. And then there was something else Anna sensed. She sensed an unfathomable mystery beginning to penetrate her heart, as if she were deeply in love. She tried to shake the feeling but it wouldn't let go of her. Then Giovanni looked up at her and smiled, and for an instant Anna was afraid he knew what she was thinking.

"You're beginning to discover something about the camino that can't be understood with your mind, Anna," he said to her. "Look around at these people. You've never met any of them, and yet you're feeling a depth of connection that can't be experienced any other place. We all walk to Assisi for different reasons, yet in the end there's really only one—to remember who we are and to realize something the Poverello always knew."

"And what is that?" Roberto asked as a profound stillness settled in around them.

"He saw something in people they couldn't see in themselves," Giovanni said. "He saw a light the world can never understand. You can call that Christ if you want or you can call it love. It doesn't really matter what words you use because they're really the same thing."

"I'm glad to hear someone say those words," a young woman named Lucia said. "The word *God* has always triggered me."

"But does the word *love* really describe God?" a young man sitting at the table asked. "I mean, the Old Testament painted a very different picture."

The conversation continued and grew more animated, but Giovanni seemed content to let it go on without his input. Anna watched him curiously, wondering if he would say anything, but he never did, at least not on the subject of God and love. He'd said his piece and seemed content letting the others wrestle with the topic.

When the meal was finished, the group settled around the fire and continued talking for hours. The other pilgrims were from Germany and spoke about their love of Italy and St. Francis, as well as their passion for walking the camino. Roberto and Michela shared stories about the many people who passed through their doors and the lessons they'd learned. Anna sat back and listened, enjoying the moment in a way she had never experienced before. For the first time since she started the journey, she felt like she was home.

11

THE WOLF OF GUBBIO

"We have a long walk ahead of us today," Giovanni said to Anna as they left their friends at Che Passo the next morning. "Most pilgrims leave Pietralunga and walk all the way to Gubbio, but our time with Michela and Roberto has put us behind schedule."

"What do you mean?" Anna asked. "I didn't realize we're on a schedule."

"What I mean is if we want to make it all the way to Gubbio and find a bed in one of the hostels."

"How far away is it?" Anna asked.

"Well, it's about fifteen kilometers to Pietralunga and then twenty-eight to Gubbio."

"That's nearly twenty-seven miles," Anna said, stopping in her tracks. "There's no way we can walk that far in one day."

"Luckily we're leaving early," he said to her, "but you're right, it's a long trek. If we keep a good pace we'll reach Gubbio by early evening. If we become tired then something will show up. Haven't you learned that lesson by now?"

Giovanni looked back at Anna and gave her a reassuring wink and she wondered if he knew something she didn't, which she thought was likely. By noon they had passed through Pietralunga. They stopped at a bar in the middle of a small village to buy sandwiches and coffee, then they were off again. Anna wanted a rest, but Giovanni was acting more like a drill sergeant than a guide. They climbed hills and passed over streams, then descended down steep paths through breathtaking forests. Anna kept her attention on her feet hoping the blisters didn't manifest again, but whatever had happened at the Eremo di Buon Riposo seemed permanent. Her feet were holding up extremely well.

By two o'clock they came to a tiny church tucked away in the forest and stopped for a short rest on a beautiful terraced courtyard overlooking the valley. Anna checked her feet—fine—and then removed a bag of granola she had bought earlier in the day, sharing it with Giovanni.

"You should probably know there are dangerous animals in the forests around Gubbio," he said matter-of-factly.

"What kind of dangerous animals?" Anna asked, nearly choking on the granola.

"Wild boars for one, and sometimes even wolves."

She looked at him wondering if he was telling her the truth, but saw no smile betray his words.

"You're telling me this now?" she said. "Have you ever seen them?"

"I've seen many boars but if you remain very still and don't behave aggressively they'll almost always leave you alone. But the wolves . . . "

Giovanni acted as if he was about to embark on a story about a dangerous encounter but then said nothing.

"Why are you stalling?" she said. "Have you seen wolves or haven't you?"

"We should get going," Giovanni said mysteriously, as he stood up and threw his small pack back over his shoulders. "We're running behind if we want to make it all the way to Gubbio."

Anna paused as she stood up. Then she grabbed her walking stick and pack and followed Giovanni into the forest. She noticed that her mind was more focused than before, looking to the left and to the right, listening for the sound of any dangerous creature that might be near.

No more than a mile later something remarkable happened. Anna and Giovanni were walking along the path when a large black wolf suddenly appeared in front of them, haunches raised as if ready to attack and a low, steady growl coming from its mouth. Anna instinctively hid behind Giovanni, grabbed hold of his arms.

"What are we going to do?" she asked him in a low, terrified voice.

Giovanni seemed as calm as ever, not at all startled by the wolf's appearance.

"We're not going to do anything," he said as he looked at her, "unless you want to meet him."

"What do you mean?" she said, her fear rising to new heights. "Can you make him go away?"

"Why would we want him to go away? This is Bevo. I see him every time I walk the camino."

"But he's a wild wolf," Anna said, slowly backing away.

"He's not so wild," Giovanni told her, "and he's not a wolf, at least not full. Maybe about half."

Giovanni walked straight up to the animal whose tail was now wagging at the sight of his friend. Bevo jumped up and began licking Giovanni's face.

"It's okay, boy," he said. "She's not really afraid of you. You did put on a very good show, though."

Anna walked closer but held a safe distance.

"You did this on purpose." she said to him. "You knew we were getting close, so you set me up with all that talk about wild animals."

"I never know when I'm going to run into Bevo, but he's always somewhere nearby."

"Doesn't he belong to anyone?" she said as she reached out her hand for Bevo to smell. "I mean, is he really tame?"

"As tame as can be," Giovanni told her. "He does look menacing so I'm not surprised you were afraid."

Bevo leaned up against Anna and his weight nearly knocked her over. He looked up at her, eager for attention.

"He really does look like a wolf," she said. "but his eyes are so soft."

"Wolves are one of the most misunderstood animals in history," Giovanni explained as they began walking again with Bevo leading the way. "Attacks are extremely rare, though there is a very famous story associated with the Poverello."

"I think I've heard it before…something about Gubbio."

"The town we're heading to now," he continued. "Of course the myth outweighs the truth."

"As usual," she said.

"I have some insight into what really happened," Giovanni said over his shoulder. "The historical sources make the wolf out to be a villain. They say he started by killing livestock and then moved on to people. Some legends say the wolf was immune to any kind of weapon and anyone who went outside the city was devoured. Of course none of that was true."

Bevo stopped suddenly and stared into the forest as if something, an animal or person, was hiding there. Giovanni and Anna looked in the same direction but saw nothing.

"Did you hear anything?" Anna asked him.

"No, but Bevo did. I trust his ears over my own."

Then he was off, running at breakneck speed, his black fur blending in with the forest floor. They heard his deep, menacing growl as it faded into the distance, and Anna found herself hoping that Bevo wasn't running toward another person, especially a child. The shock of seeing the enormous animal charging would be enough to scare someone to death. Then they could hear him barking wildly and the frantic sound of a man's voice.

"Help me! Get away . . . someone save me, please!"

Giovanni and Anna ran in the direction of the voice until they came to a small, disheveled man wearing tattered clothes who was backed against a large tree. Bevo stood only a few feet away, holding him in place.

"What's happening?" Giovanni asked as he arrived at the scene.

"What's happening? I'm about to be eaten by a wolf! Please save me!"

Giovanni walked over to Bevo who instantly reverted back to his dog-like personality. He sat down, calm as house-trained terrier. "You don't have to worry about Bevo," Giovanni told him. "He looks fierce, but it's all show. And he's not a wolf, at least not one hundred percent."

"He looks like a wolf to me," the man said as he stood up straight again. "And he growls like one too. I thought it was the end of me."

"Why are you out here?" Anna asked the man.

"I live in the forest," he told her. "I have a small hut nearby and was hunting for my dinner." He walked over to a downed tree and picked up a small rifle he had dropped during Bevo's pursuit. "That wolf is lucky I didn't use it on him . . . not that it would have mattered with his size."

"Lucky for all of us then," Giovanni said. "My friend and I are walking the Camino of St. Francis but would love to see your camp before we continue."

The man motioned for them to follow him and the companions, including Bevo the wolf-dog, walked deeper into the forest.

"My name is Frederico," he said over his shoulder. "I don't have many guests, so you'll find my home lacking." Then he stopped and turned around. "And I would be grateful if you didn't mention this to anyone. My security might be at risk if it's discovered by the wrong people."

In a few minutes they arrived at a tiny hut built out of sticks and branches with a plastic tarp draped over the top. Frederico moved an item or two and motioned for them to sit.

"I don't have anything to offer but your welcome to stay for a visit if you'd like."

"What did you mean when you said your security might be at risk?" Anna asked him as she sat down on a log next to the fire pit.

"I mean exactly what I said," he told her. "I live in the forest because there are a good number of people who are after me."

"I think Anna is asking why people are after you," Giovanni said.

Frederico looked at them as if judging whether he should tell the truth or a lie. "I have been known to take an item or two that didn't belong to me," he finally said. "I'm a thief, and quite a good one, or at least I used to be. At my age it's hard to live up to my own reputation.

"About a month ago I came across a very nice car that was left unlocked and I decided to have a look inside. I was so busy rummaging through it that I didn't hear the car's owner approach me from behind.

If I were young I would have stood my ground but his massive size convinced me to run as fast as I could. I figured the game was over since everywhere I went he was on my heels. I finally escaped here—to this very spot. I've maintained it off and on for purposes such as this."

"So you're homeless and hiding in the woods," Anna said with a note of derision.

"Whatever the case, I couldn't be happier," Giovanni said with great excitement. "It can't be a coincidence that we meet both Bevo-the-wolf-dog and Frederico-the-thief on our way to Gubbio. All of this was planned."

Hearing his name, Bevo leaned hard against Giovanni, nearly unseating him.

"I can't imagine how any of this would seem like good fortune," Frederico said.

"Haven't you heard the story of Francesco and the wolf of Gubbio?" Giovanni asked them. "I was just beginning to tell Anna the story when Bevo took off into the woods after you."

"Of course I have," Frederico answered. "I am from Gubbio. Everyone knows the tale."

"You'll have to forgive me, but I don't," Anna said. "I'm from the US."

"All right, let me finish the legend for Anna," Giovanni said. "In around 1220, when Francesco was passing through Gubbio, he heard about a wolf that was terrorizing the region. When Francesco heard the news, he decided to have a talk with the wolf. This caused a great stir, and everyone came out to watch him be eaten alive. When he neared the wolf's lair, the crowd stayed back and he continued alone. The wolf charged him full force, but the Poverello made the sign of the cross and commanded the wolf to stop. So the wolf began circling Francesco instead, waiting for an opening—but then something very interesting happened. The wolf realized Francesco wasn't afraid and started to relax. Finally, he sat down and the two had a long conversation. Francesco explained that the business of murdering innocent people and livestock couldn't continue, but there might be an alternative. If the wolf agreed to stop its evil ways, Francesco would convince the townspeople to make the wolf the town's guardian and feed him as a reward. The wolf held out its paw to seal the agreement, and a sacred contract was created. From that day on, the wolf of Gubbio watched over the village, and the villagers kept him well fed until he died two years later."

"It's a ridiculous tale," Frederico said. "Do you know how many Europeans have been killed by wolves in the last fifty years?"

"Please tell us," Giovanni said, happy he was so engaged.

"There were eight fatal attacks on the whole continent, and most of those were wolves that were rabid or wolf-dogs like your friend Bevo. Attacks by healthy, full-blooded wolves are extremely rare. Wolves stay as far away from people as possible, which is why I was so afraid when I saw your friend. I thought the European count was about to climb to nine."

"How do you know so much about wolf attacks?" Anna asked him.

"Because I am a wolf," Frederico told her. "Look at me. This is my lair, and I hunt to stay alive. I also hide from people in the village because they all want to kill me."

"As I told you before, Anna," Giovanni said mysteriously. "I have inside information about what really happened that day in 1220."

"Inside information?" Frederico exclaimed. "How did you come by it?"

"All that's important is that there never was a wolf at all," Giovanni continued. "The story was first written in a book called *The Deeds of Blessed Francis and His Brothers* around 1328, over one hundred years after Francesco died. By then, legends of the Poverello had outgrown the facts—for example, the story of the woman with withered hands that Francesco healed so she could make him a cheesecake. But the story of the wolf of Gubbio became a favorite of the people in this region."

"So what's the real story?" Anna asked.

"Believe it or not, the real wolf was very similar to our friend Frederico. He was a criminal who lived in the forest. People called him Captain Wolf because he wore an amulet that bore the image of a wolf's head. Captain Wolf was so hungry he took to stealing food and attacking people who were, as a result, terrified of him because they could never find his hiding place in the forest. Until Francesco came along. He convinced the town's people to forgive Captain Wolf's crimes if he was able to get the Captain to stop stealing and become the lookout for other bandits who might attack the town.

"Francesco found Captain Wolf hiding in a ditch. He told the Captain about the deal and made him promise to give up his old habits. Then Francesco reintroduced him to the town as Brother Lamb instead of Captain Wolf."

"Your story sounds more believable," Anna said. "Where did you read it?"

"I learned it from a reliable source," Giovanni said. Anna waited for a more satisfying answer, but it never came.

The companions stayed with Frederico a bit longer before continuing their journey to Gubbio. After so many miles, Anna wasn't sure she could walk much further, and with evening closing in, the chances of finding a suitable hostel or hotel grew less likely. And then there was the issue of Bevo. The wolf-dog seemed to have attached himself to the pair which diminished their chances of finding a room even more.

"I have the feeling we should find shelter outside of Gubbio," Giovanni said, as if reading her thoughts. "There's a barn about an hour from here where we'll be comfortable, and I'm sure we can find enough food to last us till morning."

"I never expected to be living like Frederico," Anna said to him. "But given the alternative of walking further, I'll sleep almost anywhere. Tell me more about the barn."

"It's simple, but I think you'll like it," he said. "Many pilgrims have used it in the past, and they always leave something for the comfort of the next travelers."

"You mean, like memory foam beds?"

"One never knows what the camino will provide," Giovanni told her.

The two fell into a gentle silence as they walked, Bevo panting to the side. Anna found herself thinking about everything she had experienced with her companion, from miraculously healed blisters to flocks of birds appearing out of nowhere. The thought of Giovanni walking the trails to Assisi in an endless loop, meeting and befriending emotionally distressed pilgrims along the way, was too hard to believe, yet according to Michela and Roberto it was true. Why wasn't he interested in something more, like a wife? Was it possible he was gay? He was young and charismatic, with so many gifts and opportunities; surely he must have another life other than this. And the stories he told of his family, or lack thereof, never added up. Anna's questions were mounting with every step.

"What are things like in Assisi today?" she asked him. "It's been so long since I've been there."

"In some ways, Assisi is as it has always been, as if stuck in another time," Giovanni answered. "But in other ways, it has changed a great deal as more and more tourists come. It's more commercial. But if you know where to go, you can still find the simple places where the spirits of Francesco and Chiara still exist."

"I think that's the first time you mentioned St. Clare," Anna said to him. "Isn't she as important as St. Francis?"

"Chiara has never been as popular, but yes, I would say she is just as important. She was the first woman to follow Francesco's example and she became the mother of every woman who came after her. My favorite place is the tiny church of San Damiano just below Assisi where Chiara lived with her sisters. You'll have to visit it while you're there."

"I remember it very well," Anna said to him. "When I was a little girl I used to walk down the hill and sit in the olive garden just outside the church. Sometimes my mother would take me inside. She loved kneeling next to the spot where St. Clare slept, but my favorite spot was the chapel. I felt so at home there."

"It's the first chapel the Poverello rebuilt when he heard the voice of Christ speak to him. Eight hundred years later the energy is still pure."

"When did you leave Assisi?" Anna asked, ramping up her subtle interrogation.

"You're not going to believe me if I told you," he said.

"At this point I think I'd believe almost anything."

"I left when I was eighteen to join the Esercito Italiano, the Italian army. I dreamed of being a great soldier and making my family proud of me in battle."

"I can't even imagine you as a soldier," Anna said. "There isn't any trace of it left."

"That may be true, and I'm grateful."

"Did you ever serve in a military zone?"

"Yes, but only once. It was more than enough."

"What do you mean?" she asked.

"It's not something I like to talk about. I just couldn't continue on that path, so I left."

"What do you mean you left?"

"I turned around and went home, back to Assisi. I was branded a coward and a deserter. Most of my friends turned their backs on me and I even spent a year in prison."

"I'm so sorry," Anna said as she stopped and put her hand on his arm. "What a terrible experience."

"Yes, but it broke me open."

"What do you mean?"

"God can only enter a heart that's been broken open," Giovanni said to her, his eyes gleaming in the light. "I didn't know if I could go on after that, but walking the camino and connecting with other people has been so healing. And now here I am with you. It's funny, but I've never told that story to anyone else I've walked with."

"Why did you decide to tell me?" Anna asked.

"Because you're from Assisi," he said. "We're family."

They arrived at a tiny barn set very close to the path, about a stone's throw from a small dirt road. There were no houses to be seen nor any meaningful traffic except for a young boy who rode past on a tired-looking horse. Giovanni smiled and waved, but Anna was too tired to do anything but throw off her pack and collapse on the tiny bench next to the barn.

"I never thought a barn would look like a castle," she said as she removed her shoes to inspect her feet. "Thank God they're fine."

"Thanking God is a good step," Giovanni said to her as he slid off his own pack. "Come inside. I want to show you something."

Anna slipped her shoes back on and followed him to the entrance. The door slid to the left, and the interior windows let in just enough light for her to see the inside.

"That's amazing," she said to him. "People left all that behind?"

On one side of the barn at least a hundred water containers lined the wall, and on the other side Anna saw piles of bandages, ointments, and assorted natural medicines for weary travelers. The door opened another foot, allowing enough light to reveal the back wall, which contained a huge mural showing different scenes from the camino, and just beneath the painting an assortment of paints and brushes.

"This mural has been in progress for over three years," Giovanni told her. "There's no way to know how many hands created it, but it's a tradition to add your own mark."

Anna walked to the mural and followed the path that traversed hills, through villages and many of the places that were now familiar to her. "Look, there's La Verna and the mountain that you have to climb before you get to Pieve Santo Stefano."

"Monte Calvano," Giovanni said as he stepped inside.

"That must be the Hermitage of Cerbaiolo and further on you can see the Hermitage of Montecasale. And is that who I think it is?" Anna pointed at the hooded figure of a Franciscan friar standing outside the door of the hermitage.

"Padre Nicola. Yes, that's him. You can even see him smiling."

"It's incredible," Anna said with awe. "And it's quite good."

"So many creative people walk the camino and they know how important it is to leave a part of themselves behind in gratitude. You won't find this little barn on any of the maps or guidebooks, but if you know where to look. . . ."

"I'm so grateful you brought me here," Anna said. She looked up to see the wall just beside the door where several sleeping pads rested next to what looked to be a pile of relatively clean blankets and pillows. "And look at that. We won't be on the hard ground after all."

"They may not be memory foam but they're gifts nonetheless."

A short walk to a small grocery store secured the ingredients they needed for an evening meal, and before long Giovanni had a fire started and was cooking a stew in a pot he found in the barn. Anna found plates and a box of plastic utensils and used a flat log to set a suitable table. Soon they were enjoying the meal, the moment, and the memories Anna knew she would never forget.

"Everything is given to the pilgrim who trusts Divine Providence," Giovanni said when they finished the meal.

"What exactly is Divine Providence?" Anna asked him.

"That's a good question," he answered as he looked up, thinking. "I would say it's like walking into a town with no money in your pockets knowing that every person you meet is your brother or your sister, even if it's the first time you're laying eyes on them. We're here to serve one another and know we'll be given everything we need when we do. A Divine flow starts and everyone has what they need."

"That's very hopeful but a little naïve," Anna told him.

"Why is it naïve?"

"Because most people are out to get more than their share. Look at the world we live in—the rich get richer and the poor get poorer."

"But I believe there's something within all of us that understands the truth, even though we often choose to ignore it. When we practice what I'm describing, the truth is irresistible."

"If you said that to me when we started this walk I would have said you were crazy. Now I'm not so sure."

"What's changed?" Giovanni asked her.

Anna thought about the question. When she started the journey she was angry and bitter, and every step felt like she was carrying an enormous weight. Now she felt lighter, as if she left her old life behind, along with all the grievances she had been carrying for decades.

"I'm tempted to say everything has changed," she told him. "I thought the closer I got to Assisi, the tighter I would feel. It's been just the opposite. Maybe it's the stories you've been telling me, or maybe it's St. Francis himself."

"Why do you say that?" Giovanni asked.

"It's the only thing that makes sense," she said. "I've been running away from this Poverello guy most of my life, and now I'm practically on his doorstep and feel very close to him.

"I think it's something a little deeper than that."

"Like what?" Anna asked.

"I don't know if you'll like my answer," he said.

"Maybe I will, maybe I won't, but I still want to hear it."

Giovanni looked into her eyes and she felt a warm glow envelop her. "I think it's God, however you want to define him."

"Or her," she said with a smile.

"Whichever. When you walk this path with pilgrims like the ones who painted that mural, something magical happens. All those weights we've been carrying around fall away on their own and are replaced with a feeling of grace the mind can never understand, but which your soul understands very well."

"Something else has changed," Anna said.

"What?"

"The idea of God doesn't seem to repulse me anymore. Use it whenever you want."

"Now that may be the greatest miracle yet!" Giovanni said playfully, throwing his napkin at her. Bevo snatched the napkin as it fell to the ground and ran off with it into the woods.

12

God Can Only Enter
a Broken Heart

"In two days we'll arrive in Assisi," Giovanni said to Anna as they prepared to leave the barn the next morning. "We're going to pass through Gubbio and walk to Biscina Castle. There are so many great things to see in Gubbio, though, and I recommend you return when you can."

"There's no need," Anna said to him. "We visited Gubbio many times when I was a child. I even saw the candle race once." She remembered the huge wooden candles being carried through the town and the crowds of people lining the streets all the way to the main church. "I couldn't move, there were so many people. I remember feeling crushed by everyone there shouting encouragement to the three racers. Those candles were at least twenty feet long, if I remember. They must have weighed a ton."

"Which is why carrying them is a sign of manhood. When the races started, back in the twelfth century, it was meant to celebrate a kind of military victory. Each of the candles is topped with a statue of a saint that relates to a part of the town, and a man from each part carries their saint's candle to the roar of the crowd."

"I don't really like crowds," Anna said as she stuffed her clothes into her backpack.

"Then there's a story you might like of the Poverello fleeing to Gubbio when he first rejected his father's wealth. He found a former friend who lived there, and was given a simple peasant's tunic to wear while serving the lepers just outside of town. That tunic became the habit Franciscans have been wearing for eight hundred years.

"The thought of going back to Assisi to be around throngs of people made Francesco feel empty, but being with the lepers and living a simple life as Christ did filled him with joy. I think it's the same for me walking the camino. Walking with just one or two people makes me feel better than walking with two hundred. When we're broken open we see what's important and what isn't, and it's the simple things that make us feel closest to God and to each other."

"There's one thing I need to do before we leave," Anna said.

Bevo waited patiently outside the door, ready to begin walking, while Anna headed to the back wall, where the mural reflected the morning sun. She took a brush, dipped it in paint, and wrote the words: "God can only enter the heart that has been broken open." Then she cleaned the brush, threw the pack over her shoulder, and was ready to leave.

"Now we can go," she said.

The sight of the enormous wolf-dog walking beside Anna and Giovanni caused some alarm along the road to Gubbio, especially when they passed the statue commemorating the fabled storyline on the outskirts of town. The wolf depicted jumping into St. Francis's arms, however, was much smaller than Bevo—more like a medium-sized German shepherd. Bevo, with his wild and brutish appearance, matched the fable to an uncomfortable degree, and several people moved to the opposite side of the road when they spotted the trio. A few people even seemed paralyzed. Anna found the spectacle amusing and more than once reached her hand down to pet the animal, especially when she knew the others were watching.

"Notice how afraid everyone is?" Anna said to Giovanni. "It's like the legend just became reality."

"Bevo is so gentle. If they only knew, they wouldn't be so scared."

"How far is it to Biscina?" she asked.

"Twenty-two kilometers," he told her. "Right now, we're walking along what's called the Franciscan Path of Peace. Did you know that the Poverello was one of the first interreligious peacemakers?"

"I have a vague memory about him trying to end the Crusades by going to meet the sultan."

"Exactly. He thought he could convert the sultan and end the war if he was able to share the true message of Jesus."

"As opposed to what, the false message?"

"It depends on who you ask," Giovanni said. "To Francesco the message of Jesus had nothing to do with battles and war. It was about peace. He thought that if he could share the gospel of peace with the sultan he would end the war on his own."

"It didn't work, did it?"

"Once again, it depends on who you ask. Sultan Malik al-Kamil was so impressed by the crazy mystic wandering into his camp that he gave Francesco an audience. He was moved by Francesco's simplicity and his love of God. The sultan also had a great love of God. He had the spirit of a true Sufi, which is much like the spirit of a true Franciscan. Since then, there has been a peaceful energy between the Franciscan order and most Muslims."

"That must have ruffled a few feathers," Anna said.

"It still does," Giovanni said. "In 1986, Pope John Paul II decided to invite leaders from the twelve major religions of the world to Assisi to pray for peace together. You wouldn't believe how angry it made many of the bishops and cardinals. They begged him not to go through with the event, but the Pope was very much like the Poverello—he didn't care what other people thought, only what Jesus thought. Because of the special relationship between St. Francis and the sultan, Muslim leaders were happy to attend. You should have seen it, Anna. Each religious group was given a chapel or a sacred place in Assisi to conduct their ceremonies and then they all gathered at the basilica. Each one of them prayed the peace prayer from their own religion. Francesco would have been so happy to see this happen in his town."

They climbed up and down green hills that day, passing the road that lead to the Abbey of Vallingegno and later the Hermitage of San Pietro in Vigneto. Giovanni instructed Anna to be silent when they walked past the hermitage. "The hermit who maintains this holy place is always in prayer and doesn't like to be disturbed," he said.

They climbed a gentle path up a dirt road, and when they came to its end, took a left turn. In front of them, set atop a lovely green hill, they saw Biscina Castle, where they decided to spend the night.

"After sleeping in the barn last night, this looks like a palace," Anna said.

"Unfortunately, the castle is not open, but there is a very nice guest house," Giovanni told her. "I wanted our last night before arriving in Assisi to be special. It's actually a working farm, or what we call an "agriturismo," built in the twelfth century but badly damaged by an earthquake in 1984. They've done a great job restoring it to its original condition."

They climbed the hill until they reached the entrance. Once inside, Anna saw a pretty young woman behind a small desk who lit up when she saw Giovanni.

"You're back," she said, standing and coming out to greet them—until she saw Bevo and froze in place.

"Lucia, this is my friend Anna," Giovanni said to her, "and the dog is Bevo. Don't worry, he will stay outdoors."

Giovanni's quick motion to Bevo was so slight Anna barely noticed it, but the dog immediately darted outside. Lucia appeared relieved.

"Well, I'm very happy to see you," she said to Giovanni, barely glancing at Anna. "How long has it been, two months?"

Anna smiled as she watched the interaction. This was clearly a woman with a crush. Lucia began to flush as she spoke, but Giovanni didn't seem to notice.

"Maybe three," Giovanni said to her. "I would never come to this area without visiting your beautiful castle and, of course, you, Lucia." She reached out and touched his hand, and Giovanni didn't hesitate to take it into his own.

"Do you have two rooms for the night? And if you do, the nicest is for Anna." Lucia looked at Anna for the first time, as if recovering from a spell.

"Yes, of course," she said, regaining her composure and rushing back behind her desk. "The best room is still available, and your favorite room as well, Giovanni." Giovanni smiled and Anna let the pack slide off her back.

It was nearly time for dinner when Anna entered her room in one of the guest buildings near the castle. It was simple yet stately. The high ceilings and enormous archways made her feel like a princess locked in a medieval castle guarded day and night by a king too afraid to let her set foot outside the fortress on her own. Unable to shake the strange image, she unpacked and then sat on the bed, looking around and wondering if the impression came from a dream or some half-buried childhood memory. Her own father had been overprotective and controlling, and when she was small she had thought it meant he loved her. But as a teenager his domineering energy had overwhelmed her own, pushing her to the point of rebelliousness. At the thought of her father, tears formed in the corners of her eyes and before long she was sobbing into her pillow. The closer she came to Assisi and the possibility of seeing her father again, the stronger her emotions became and the more vulnerable she felt.

Anna found Giovanni sitting in the dining room drinking a glass of wine. His eyes were closed as if deep in meditation, and as Anna sat down at the table he didn't move at all. She waited for him, and after at least two minutes he opened his eyes.

"I didn't hear you come," he said to her as he shook himself slightly. "I was so deep in my prayer."

"You look more tired than me," she said to him.

"I'm not tired at all," Giovanni answered. "This castle brings back so many memories."

"The young lady must be one of them," Anna said. "Lucia is her name?"

"Lucia is an amazing woman."

"Maybe she's the reason you like staying here," Anna suggested smiling knowingly.

"I'm attracted to her the same way I'm attracted to you or anyone else," he answered, realizing what she was hinting at. "I'm attracted to the light in her."

"Ah, I see," Anna said, not sure whether she should believe him or not. "No romance for you, right?"

Giovanni smiled at her but did not answer the question. Why was he hiding this part of his life from her? Was he so cut off from the world that he didn't even think of women or relationships? If not, why did he spend all his time walking to Assisi with a woman nearly three times his age when so many younger women were clearly interested in him?

A young man stepped up to the table and asked Anna if she wanted anything to drink. She motioned that she would have the same as Giovanni, then turned back to Giovanni and said:

"So, tomorrow we arrive in Assisi. Where will you go when you get there?"

"I haven't decided yet. And you?"

Anna hesitated. She wasn't sure she was ready to tell him about her desire to see her father. There was no way of knowing if he was even there. She had seen a picture of him posing as a distant cousin of St. Francis on an Italian website four years earlier, standing next to an English woman. "Up to his old tricks," she had thought at the time. But that didn't mean he was still alive. And now there was just no way of knowing until she arrived.

"I'm going to look up a friend or two," she told him. "It'll feel strange being there after so many years."

"And what about your father?" Giovanni asked.

Anna was silent. She was losing track of the times he seemed to jump right to her innermost thoughts from the most vulnerable part of her life, but it was still shocking.

"What do you mean?" she asked him hoping to deflect the conversation as quickly as possible. "Did Michela say something to you?"

"No, she didn't say anything. Aren't you hoping to find him? That's the reason you're going to Assisi, yes?"

From out of nowhere, Anna felt a great anger erupt inside her. She felt violated, meddled with. After all the conversations about her life in Assisi and troubled relationship with her father, it was an easy jump to make, but the suddenness of his breach unnerved her.

"Why would you say that?" she said, stiffening in her chair. "Presuming he's even alive, what makes you think I would walk all this way to see a man who turned me away when I was a child?"

"I'm sorry if my question seemed intrusive," Giovanni said.

"Intrusive? Try invasive. You've been invading my mind since we met and I don't like it at all. I don't know if you're just extremely intuitive or if all your spiritual mumbo jumbo has turned you into a psychic, but it has to stop."

"Anna, I didn't mean. . . ."

"Sure you did," Anna said as she stood up from the table. "I don't know why you're so interested in what happens to me after tomorrow, but you don't have to be. I'm sure I can find my way from here. Only one day left, right?"

"Don't leave, Anna," Giovanni pleaded.

"Don't leave the guesthouse, or don't leave you? What would happen if I did leave you, Giovanni? Are you only happy when you have a broken lamb like me tagging along after you? Does that give you the chance to play the guru, when in reality you're just as scared as I am? I don't know what your deal is, but I think I've had enough. Don't look for me in the morning. I still have my guidebook. I'll find the way on my own."

Giovanni looked at her helplessly as Anna turned and stormed away, passing the waiter who was bringing her wine.

An hour later she lay in bed looking up at the ceiling, still brooding. She considered calling a taxi and going to Assisi that very night, showing up at her father's house and finally confronting her fears. She was only fifteen miles away, so close she almost could feel the gravitational pull of her former home. But she knew she would regret not finishing the camino. Even if she walked alone—which she had already decided—at least she would march into the town with her head held high. She would find the house and knock on the door, then see the look on her father's face when his daughter's apparition materialized before him. She wanted to see his shock turn to agonizing remorse as he remembered what he had done. Then she would turn around and walk away, satisfied she'd had the last word.

Anna turned off the light and closed her eyes. Dreams evaded her sleep that night, and she was happy for it.

τ

The next morning, Anna rose early and prepared to leave before seeing Giovanni and even without having her camino credential stamped. It was 6:30 AM when she left the castle. As she walked down the drive that led to the small road, she looked for Bevo. Determined as she was to leave Giovanni behind, Anna hoped the wolf-dog would still accompany her. She called out to him, but only the sound of the birds singing praise to the morning sun answered. Disappointed, she walked to the path and started the final approach to Assisi.

With the guidebook in hand Anna navigated her way along the paths and small dirt roads, past two ruined houses and what looked like neglected cemeteries. Before long she found herself walking beside a charming river amid rich meadows and dense thickets. She passed through the town of Valfabbrica and then climbed steep hills on her way to Pieve San Nicolò.

Her pack was growing heavy as she ascended the hills, which became increasingly treacherous. Anna wiped the sweat away from her eyes as she walked, her weariness soon distracting her from the map. Somewhere along the way she made a wrong turn, and Anna realized she was lost. Nothing in the guidebook corresponded with what she was seeing. The question was, should she keep going or turn back? In despair, Anna threw off her pack and collapsed on the ground.

"What am I doing out here?" she screamed. In response, she was greeted with silence, and felt encouraged to release. "Why am I here? What the hell did I think was going to happen?"

She stood up and kicked her pack, which slid into the ditch. She picked up the walking stick, ready to break it in half but for the memory of Sister Celeste. Instead, she tossed it lightly to the spot where the pack landed, then picked up a rock and threw it as hard as she could. "Why did I think walking this stupid camino would change anything? He threw me out and that's the end. Why are you trying to go back, Anna? What are you hoping to accomplish?"

By now, Anna was screaming so loud she didn't hear the sound of the wolf-dog's huge paws running toward her. Almost before she had a moment to be shocked, Bevo was in her lap, licking her face.

"Bevo, I thought I lost you!" she said, overjoyed to see her friend.

"And you thought you lost me as well," she heard a voice say. Anna turned and saw Giovanni standing at the side of the road smiling at her. For a second, surprise had the best of her, but then she realized how much she had missed her companion. She ran to him and threw her arms around him.

"Oh, Giovanni, I am so happy to see you," Anna said.

Giovanni held her in his arms and Bevo jumped up, pushing his way into the middle. She pulled back and looked at him. "I'm so sorry for what I said last night," she said, tears rolling down her cheeks. "The closer I get to Assisi the more afraid I am. You were right—I'm hoping my father is still alive and I get one last chance to see him. I don't even care what he did or how I felt all these years. I just want to see him and tell him I still love him."

"Then we should get going," Giovanni said to her. "You're pretty far off the path, you know."

"I just realized that. How did you know where . . . actually, never mind. I've given up trying to figure you out, Giovanni. I'm giving up on that damn guidebook and following wherever you lead me."

Anna pulled the pack over her shoulder, grabbed her walking stick, and began retracing her steps with Giovanni in the lead.

"It was right around here somewhere that Francesco got turned around once," he said to her.

"Why am I not surprised?"

"Unfortunately for him, he didn't meet a friend to lead him back in the right direction. It wasn't long after his conversion in Assisi, and he was filled with joy to the point of foolishness. He was dancing and singing in French when he came across a group of bandits."

"Let me guess, he had nothing for them to rob so they left him alone."

"Yes and no," Giovanni continued. "The robbers recognized him as the son of a rich Assisian, Pietro Bernardone, though the clothes he was wearing didn't match how they remembered him. When they asked Francesco who he was he said, 'I am the herald of the great king. What is it to you?' The bandits didn't like that answer, so they grabbed him, searched him, and when they didn't find anything to steal they beat him and threw him into the ravine. 'Lie there, you clownish herald of God,' they yelled as they left. Francesco was overjoyed by the men's treatment. He got back up, brushed off the snow and dirt, and started singing and dancing again as he continued his journey."

"I just don't understand the stories you tell me," Anna said to him. "Why is it considered a victory when he's beaten and abused, and then he goes on singing like a simpleton?"

Giovanni stopped walking and turned to face her with eyes so bright Anna felt the need to turn away.

"You have to remember that Francesco had been treated like royalty in Assisi all of his life. As the son of a rich merchant he had everything a young man could ever want—the finest clothes, money, and even women. When he left all that behind, he wanted to be treated like any other poor person, because he wanted to identify himself completely with the homeless Christ. He was drunk on the love of God, which, by the way, is the best intoxicant in the world. Being beaten and abused didn't interrupt his joy, it made him feel richer than he ever felt when he had money and prestige."

"Have you ever been beaten walking the camino?" Anna asked him.

"What made you think of that?"

"I don't know . . . you and St. Francis are so alike. I thought maybe you had a similar experience."

"I was robbed once by a young boy," he said, dipping his head.

"A young boy?"

"Yes, it's embarrassing, but I didn't have the heart to turn him away."

"What do you mean?" she asked. "He was robbing you."

"All he had was a rusty old knife, but I felt bad, so I gave him what little money I had and sent him on his way. The next time I was walking the camino I saw him in Casella del Ponte, just a few miles behind us. I don't think he recognized me, but I definitely recognized him. He was helping an old lady carry wood through the village. I had to wonder if he had left his robbing days behind."

"I wouldn't be surprised," Anna said. "One encounter with you and anything could happen."

Two hours later, Anna, Giovanni, and Bevo were walking along a dirt road and climbing a difficult hill when Giovanni stopped and suddenly became very serious.

"Anna, I want you to do something for me when you arrive in Assisi," he said.

"Where will you be?" Anna asked him.

"Just in case we get separated when we get inside the city walls, it's important that you go straight to the basilica and visit the tomb of the Poverello. It has to be the first thing you do. Then I want you to visit the chapel of San Damiano where Santa Chiara lived."

"Why is it so important?"

"Ending the camino at the tomb is tradition," Giovanni explained. "Whenever a pilgrim finishes the camino they go there and give thanks for a safe journey. You're going to be overwhelmed when you first arrive, so it's important you don't forget."

"And what about San Damiano?"

"You said you loved going there as a child," he said to her. "It may bring the healing you're looking for."

Anna wasn't sure how to respond to the strange instructions. Was he intending to turn around as soon as they arrived in Assisi and return to La Verna to find his next lost sheep?

"But we're going to be together when we arrive so you'll remind me," she said to him.

"Just in case," he said. "Make sure you go to both places straight away."

They started walking again. Anna stared thoughtfully at his back as she followed with Bevo far up ahead.

13

THE FINAL APPROACH

As they crested a hill, Giovanni pointed at Mount Subasio, the mountain on which Assisi had been built two thousand years earlier. The sight of it filled Anna with unexpected euphoria. This was her playground when she was a child. She remembered hiking to the top with her mother, straight into the clouds that hung above the valley like a white blanket. She was finally home, and that feeling was expanding with each step. Anna found herself walking faster, ahead of both Giovanni and Bevo now, as if pulled by an invisible force. Several more hills, and it was almost in sight—the town of her dreams and deepest longing. She was almost running as she topped the last hill and saw the steeple of the Basilica di San Francesco and the Rocca Maggiore, the highest part of Assisi, rise in front of her.

The sight took her breath away.

Standing on the hill looking at the town of her birth, something unexpected stirred within Anna. This was her village, the home of her ancestors and childhood friends. At that moment she realized just how much she had yearned to return. She had pushed it away for so long it now appeared like a vision through the mist, clinging to the side of Mount Subasio like an infant held tight in her mother's arms.

The memory of her own mother came rushing back, and Anna felt a terrible stab in her heart. Why had she waited so long? Why hadn't she come the moment she had heard her mother was ill, so many years ago?

Was it to spite her father, whose heavy hand pushed her away, loving his honor more than a daughter who could never live up to the family crest? If she had come then, forty years earlier, perhaps she could have healed her mother. Perhaps it was the balm she needed, her only daughter at her side. But Anna hadn't come, and no matter how many years passed, she couldn't forgive herself.

Maybe she was more like her father than she had thought. Was she protecting her own honor when her mother needed her most? At what cost? But she was too stubborn. Too angry. She wouldn't give her father the satisfaction.

It all came flooding back as Anna stood looking at the basilica, her accuser, which pierced the sky like a finger pointing directly at her. St. Francis's body was entombed there, the central figure in this drama. But even if it was true, even if her family was related to the saint, what difference did it make? All it had done was force Anna away from her mother, the one person who might have saved her during those early rebellious years.

For a moment Anna didn't know if she could continue. Part of her wanted to throw her pack in the ditch and launch the walking stick into the brush, then find the nearest train station. She could escape to Rome and smother her sadness in whatever vice she wanted—fine restaurants, expensive wine, cigarettes, and anything else that came into her mind. But what would she feel when the intoxication wore off? Would the sorrow come rushing back, reminding her of what she had lost, or would the chapter close without climax, depositing her back to her life in Portland as easily as it had led her away?

She looked again at the village in front of her, the one that had given her so much joy as a child. She remembered when her mother had brought her to the tomb, and they knelt there together, asking to be made into instruments of peace. She remembered her father's stories about St. Francis and how wonderful it was to be related to him. "Something to be proud of," he would say, "and something to live up to." As a young girl, such ideas had inspired her but, later, when she felt herself slipping toward adolescent disdain, the stories seemed ridiculous, even something to be ashamed of. She had pushed her family away like Francis had rejected the lepers he encountered in his early life, before his transformation. When everything changed for him, the thing he found most horrid transformed into such sweetness. Would the same thing happen for her now? Would the village and life she rejected become the source of a sweetness greater than she could have imagined?

"Isn't it beautiful?" she said to Giovanni. Anna turned to look at him, to see if he was as moved as she was, but realized she was alone. She turned and looked behind her, wondering if he and Bevo had fallen back to give her space, or even dashed behind a bush for privacy. "What a strange moment to pick," Anna thought. This was the moment of triumph, the final reward after so many steps and so many tears. She looked in every direction, but Giovanni was nowhere to be seen.

"Giovanni . . . where are you? Bevo?"

Only the sound of the wind blowing through the trees greeted her. In the distance she could hear cars and buses climbing the hill to the village, and the distant sound of church bells filled the air. But where were her companions? Had they slipped away on purpose, giving her the chance to feel the depths of the moment on her own? She wished she had told Giovanni this was something she had wanted to share, since without him she would have never made it this far.

Minutes turned into an hour, and Anna realized she had to continue alone. The thought that he had turned back to La Verna filled her with a loneliness she didn't expect. But after taking a final breath, Anna began walking in the direction of Assisi anyway.

She descended the hill, turning left at the statue of the Franciscan Saint Padre Pio, the floating saint Giovanni had told her about, and then climbed a long hill up to a charming bridge. Then she finally saw it: St. James Gate. This would be the final approach since the gate was only a short distance from the basilica.

Why did Giovanni stress visiting the tomb of St. Francis as soon as she arrived in Assisi? Anna knew it was the traditional first stop, but it now it felt as if he knew she would be alone when she entered the town. She saw the medieval stone gate ahead of her, and everything she had been holding back hit her full force. She stepped through the gate, then took a deep gulp of air.

"You never thought you'd see me again, did you?" she asked as she looked around at the familiar sights. "Well, here I am."

The buildings hadn't changed in hundreds of years, and Anna wasn't surprised to see familiar faces staring back at her through shop doors and half-shuttered windows. They wouldn't recognize her—she was sure of it. When she had left Assisi she was little more than a child. Almost immediately she noticed a woman around her age waiting tables in a small café that had always been managed by a former schoolmate's family. She wondered if this really was her friend hiding beneath years of service. Anna shielded her face to avoid being recognized and continued walking toward the basilica.

It felt like a dream. Tourists wandered past Anna just as they did when she was young, visiting churches and shops that sold an infinite supply of holy medals and plaster statues. An old woman stepped onto a second-floor balcony and shook a small rug, sending dust into the air. She looked down at Anna curiously. The backpack and walking stick must give her the appearance of an ordinary pilgrim walking from La Verna, but the old woman stared longer than usual, as if she could see beneath the mask to the young girl who had walked the same streets decades earlier. Then she disappeared back inside. Perhaps it was all Anna's imagination, but it startled her nonetheless. Everywhere she looked she saw familiar faces, and she wondered if they saw her as well.

Then she turned a corner and saw it—the Basilica di San Francesco. Anna stopped and held her breath, the effect was so strong. She remembered the lessons every child from Assisi learned—that construction of the impressive structure started in 1228, only two years after St. Francis's death, and comprised two levels known as the Upper Church and the Lower Church. The crypt, where she was headed now, along with countless others, was buried beneath the Lower Church like a forgotten room, with no windows or external light, lit only by dim bulbs and tall candles. Both sections were decorated with frescoes by numerous late medieval painters from the Roman and Tuscan schools, including works by Cimabue, Simone Martini, Pietro Lorenzetti, Pietro Cavallini and the greatest of them all—Giotto. How strange that the man who wanted to live like the birds of the air would have such a monument built in his honor. Anna was sure St. Francis would have been horrified.

She entered the Lower Church and wondered if her appearance would draw attention. She was covered in the dust of countless trails, and Anna was surprised when the friar sitting nearest the door looked at her lazily, then looked away. As soon as she saw the simple staircase that led to the crypt, Anna turned left, almost sure she felt her mother's presence walking beside her. She instinctively held out her hand, as if reaching for her, then walked until she stood at the top of the stairs. Several people pushed past her, anxious to visit the tomb, but Anna hesitated. Once she walked down the stone steps, her time on the Camino would be over, and she wasn't sure she wanted it. "Giovanni should be at my side," she couldn't help thinking. He was the one who had inspired her to keep walking even when she wanted to abandon the path. He should be with her now that she had made it, but he was not.

Anna felt the air cool as she walked slowly down the steps. Then she saw the tomb just ahead of her, perched above a simple altar behind metal grating, nearly invisible inside the huge column where the saint's bones had been hidden for so many centuries. Around and behind the column, Anna saw the other tombs where the first companions were buried. Overhead, in the main church, priceless frescoes covered the walls, but here, in this simple place, was only this humble testament to a man who had changed the world.

Anna was swept into the stream of people trying to get closer to the tomb. She saw an opening and slipped into one of the pews. She didn't remember so many people cramming the small space when she was young and began to feel her chest tightening. But despite that, she felt something, a vibration similar to the energy she had sensed when she lay upon the stone bed in the Eremo di Montecasale. If not for that, she would have turned around and escaped, but the feeling held her in place.

Though there were at least one hundred people in the chapel, it was completely silent. Anna closed her eyes. She couldn't shake the vibration she felt deep within, as if a door was opening that had been closed for so long. The wider the door opened, the stronger the vibration became until Anna wondered if she would be able to stand it. She felt a tear form in the corner of her eye, and wiped it away before it could begin its long fall down her cheek.

Then Anna felt a hand holding her own. She opened her eyes, expecting to see Giovanni sitting next to her, but there was no one there. She looked down at her hand, fist clenched in a tight ball. "It just my imagination," she told herself, closing her eyes again and trying to force the vibration away. Instead, she heard a voice, not so much with her ears but deep inside of her heart. It spoke softly, as if in a whisper, but the words were clear and resonant: "I am always with you, my child."

Her mother's voice. Anna knew it was real. This was not an apparition but a kind of echo, as if the voice had been bouncing off the walls of the tiny chapel for decades waiting for this moment when she would be sitting in this very spot, the very place where they had sat together so long before.

"Never forget how much I love you," the voice said. "I have never left you."

Anna put her hands to her face and began to weep. The years and decades of guilt came rushing forward lifting her above the waves of grief and loneliness to a place she couldn't quite recognize but had longed to know. Her mother forgave her. That was all she knew. If she had walked the entire Camino for this single moment, it had been worth every step.

Anna looked up at the tomb with deep gratitude.

"*Grazie*, Francesco," she whispered. "Thank you."

14

HER FATHER'S HOUSE

When Anna left the basilica, something had shifted inside her. She felt like she had been carrying a backpack filled with rocks for years and even when she forgot it was there she still felt the oppressive weight. Now she was free. Whether she had imagined her mother's hand and voice in the basilica's crypt or it was real didn't matter at that moment. For the first time in decades she sensed something that felt like faith—not in something that was outside her but in something so intimate and real it was impossible to deny.

But she had one more stop to make before her journey was complete, even before following Giovanni's instructions to visit the chapel at San Damiano. Anna reached into her pocket and took out the wrinkled slip of paper she had been carrying since she left Portland. *Renaldo B., Via Eremo delle Carceri #5, Assisi.* As she looked at the paper, a familiar heaviness returned to her heart. This was the reason she had come back to Assisi. Every step she had taken was in the direction of this address.

There was no reason to prolong her final move. She started walking toward upper Assisi, the place where her time on the Camino of St. Francis would truly end. Her anger towards her father had given way to compassion. When she had started the camino she'd had no idea what she would say when she saw her father after so many decades. Perhaps a few angry words before walking away forever. Now all she wanted to do was wrap her arms around him and cry, not only for the mother she lost but for the ocean that separated them since she was a child. As she walked, she noticed how different she felt and how happy she was to be home again. "Home again." The words felt so strange swimming through her mind, but it was true. She was a Bernardone—just like St. Francis—and this was where her heart would always remain.

Anna had forgotten how steep the roads were that led toward the Basilica of Santa Chiara. She had been a child when she left Assisi and climbing these hills was nothing. But the years had softened her, and if it hadn't been for the mountains Anna had already climbed through Tuscany and Umbria she may not have made it. But the camino had given her strength and confidence.

As she walked up Via San Francesco she passed many more places she recognized—hotels, pizzerias, and the homes of people she once knew. Some had changed and many were just as they were when she left, exactly as they had been for hundreds of years. She saw museums and tourist shops had sprung up over the decades to serve the five million visitors that come to Assisi each year.

As she came to the Piazza del Comune, Assisi's main square, more memories flooded back. In one corner, just off the piazza, a small church marked the spot where St. Francis's house once stood. On the other side was a two-thousand-year-old Roman temple for the goddess Minerva. Just ahead, Anna saw the road that led up the hill toward Via Eremo delle Carceri, the street where she would finally end her walk. Someone was waiting for her there, though there was no way he could know she was coming. Anna felt uncertain, but still she turned left, passing the pharmacy, then walked up the steep hill, past St. Rufino's church, before finally coming to the outdoor parking lot where she could nearly see her destination.

Anna looked up the hill and saw a row of houses, and just for a second she considered ending her journey where she was. "Even if he's there, what's the point of going through with it?" she thought. "It might cause more harm than good." But she knew she had to. There was no turning back now. She couldn't stop a block from her father's house.

Her feet felt like lead weights as she walked on the sidewalk just beside the parking lot. Her eyes were focused on the house, on the windows and door. What if he stepped outside that very moment? He would be seventy-eight, or seventy-nine perhaps, and it was possible he never left the house at all. But he would be there. She was sure of it. He was waiting for her just as she had been waiting for this moment to arrive.

All at once she was at the house. She stood looking at the door. Then she slid the backpack from her shoulder and laid the walking stick against the open stone gate. Anna walked to the door, then hesitated again. "Will he even recognize me?" she wondered. What if he saw her standing at the door and thought she was a neighbor or a lost tourist? Would he send her away without a second glance? Did he still consider it his role to represent the Bernardone family—the ancestors of St. Francis? Or were those antics in the past? Perhaps he was now reduced to an old man with nothing better to do than sit alone in a house she wouldn't even recognize.

Of course, this wasn't the house Anna had been raised in. That was on the other side of town. She heard that he had sold it when her mother died and moved to one more suited for a single man. A single man. Is that what he was? Had he remained unmarried all this time? Anna had no idea what her father's life was like after so many decades. Anything could have happened. Anything.

She knocked on the ancient door, her feet shifting nervously beneath her as she listened for the slow shuffling feet of an old man coming to answer. She heard nothing. Anna knocked again, almost hoping he wasn't there. Then she could say she tried, that she went to the house, but he wasn't home. She had completed her journey, and that was enough.

But then she heard something. Footsteps were moving in her direction, and Anna felt herself stand straighter, as if she was a child again and needed her father's approval. Anna heard the lock being opened and the door handle began to turn. A woman in her mid-thirties with short brown hair slowly opened the door.

"Can I help you?" she asked in Italian.

The woman's voice was soft and sweet, and Anna didn't know what to say. She wasn't prepared for this—someone other than her father opening the door. She cleared her throat.

"Si, I'm looking for Renaldo Bernardone. Is he here?"

The woman's smile disappeared. "Renaldo?" the woman said. "Can I ask why you're looking for him?"

The question shook Anna's confidence. What difference did it make? Was this a nurse or a house maid? What right did she have to ask?

"It's personal," Anna answered. "I've come a very long distance to see him."

"You're American," the woman said, "but also Italian. I can tell by your accent. But once again I must ask what this is in regard to."

For the first time, Anna realized that she didn't know why she was there. She knew that she had to see her father again, and that was all. She had looked online and found that Assisi website article and picture, but the post was four years old. A week later, the camino guidebook had fallen off the shelf and hit her on the head. Deep down, she hoped there still might a chance . . . for what? Was she really going to heal all those wounds from childhood? Did she just want to look at him one last time and forgive him? It was a thought that hadn't occurred to her until she had spent time with Giovanni. He was the change in climate that melted her heart to the point that she was ready to release her father, to look him in his eyes and tell him all the things she longed to say. But she had to approach him slowly, and walking one hundred and ten miles through the mountains of Tuscany and Umbria would be the perfect way.

"I'm sorry," Anna said, "but it really is personal. Is he here?"

The woman's smile softened and her dark eyes grew cloudy with unexpected tears. It was only then that Anna realized she was more than a nurse or a house maid. Perhaps she was a relative, a cousin or a niece, someone Anna couldn't have known.

"I'm very sorry," the woman finally said, "but he passed away two years ago. I lived here with him before . . . before he died, and I thought it was best to hold onto it . . . the house, I mean."

Anna felt her knees buckle beneath her. She reached out for the door frame and steadied herself, then took a long, deep breath. The earth seemed to be moving beneath her, and she couldn't seem to regain her balance.

"I'm so sorry," Anna said in a near whisper. "I didn't mean to trouble you. Thank you for letting me know."

She turned and walked to her backpack and walking stick. It was over. After decades of wondering what had happened to her family and hoping one day to return, there was nothing left. Assisi was now in her past and she could return to Portland in relative peace. At least she knew. There would be no more wondering. She picked up the pack and threw it over her shoulder.

The woman was still standing in the door watching Anna, as if looking for clues about why she would be looking for Renaldo Bernardone and why she was so overwhelmed by the news of his death.

"Maybe there's something I can do to help you," she said as she took a step toward Anna. Anna stopped, turning to tell the woman that there was nothing she could do when the woman said, "You see, Renaldo was my father."

"Your father? What do you mean?"

"I mean he was my father."

Was it possible? Was this her sister? Anna had assumed he'd spent the rest of his life alone. Had he remarried and lived a life she had never even imagined?

"What is your name?" Anna asked.

"Marisa. My mother died eight years ago, but I stayed near my father because he needed me. He needed someone, and no one else cared for him like I did."

Anna looked at the woman and suddenly saw her father's eyes looking back at her. They were dark and beautiful just as his were, and her features were similar to her own. It was true. She had a sister.

Anna walked back to the door and threw her arms around Marisa as tears poured from her eyes.

"Oh my God, I'm your sister," Anna cried.

Marisa tried to push Anna away, until the news seemed to sink in, and she returned Anna's embrace.

"You're Anna?" Marisa said as she pulled back to look into her eyes. "You're my sister? I've wanted to meet you my entire life."

"You knew about me?" Anna said as she wiped away her tears. "My father spoke about me?"

"Of course he did. All the time."

Marisa took Anna by the hand and led her into the house. Next to the window, Anna saw a bookshelf filled with framed photographs. In the center, she noticed a large picture of a young girl around sixteen. It was her, perhaps a few months before she left for the US. There were other pictures of Anna and her mother, as well as pictures of a younger Marisa and a woman Anna assumed was Marisa's mother. But the one in the center was most prominent.

"He had this the entire time?" Anna said, as overwhelming joy engulfed her. She picked up the photo and looked into the eyes of her younger self, remembering how innocent and filled with faith she was. Then she looked at the other photos—mother, her parent's wedding pictures, and many more of her. For the first time since she was a child, Anna felt like she was part of a great and ancient family.

"He loved the one you're holding," Marisa said. "He used to stare at it for hours dreaming you would come home one day. I tried to track you down but couldn't find a trace."

"My married name," she said through her tears. "You would have had to know my married name."

"Yes, I thought of that. I had given up hope, but here you are."

"Were these the only pictures he had of me?" Anna asked her.

Marisa reached beneath a small table next to the bookshelf and pulled out a shoebox. When she opened it, Anna saw it was stuffed with photos. Marisa poured them onto the floor, and Anna saw picture after picture from her childhood. There were dozens of photos of her when she was a baby as well and many more from her youth. But there was one that stood out—a photograph of Anna, aged twelve or thirteen, and her mother standing in front of the Basilica di San Francesco. And she was holding her mother's hand, exactly as she had in her dream the night before she started the camino.

"I dreamed about this," she said. "My mother and I used to go to the basilica and pray at the tomb. It inspired me so much, but after I left Italy everything changed." Then Anna looked at her sister and touched her face with her hand. "Do you realize I have a daughter older than you?"

Marisa took Anna's hand into her own and smiled.

"I always knew. Papa talked about it all the time. I wish you could have been here and seen how he changed. I know it was hard for you when you were young, but when your mother died, he softened." Then, as if suddenly realizing the gravity of the visit, she said: "And how in the world did you get here . . . to Assisi and this house?"

"I walked."

15

SAN DAMIANO

Anna knelt in the tiny chapel of San Damiano, a short walk below Assisi on the lower slope of Mount Subasio. This was the spot where St. Francis had founded his ministry after witnessing a miracle: The cross above the altar had come to life, and Jesus had spoken to Francis, giving him his first mission—to rebuild the church which was falling to ruin. At the time, he had thought it meant the chapel where Anna now sat, which had been beaten down and forgotten, but later he realized that Christ had meant something much bigger: Francesco was to rebuild the entire church, which at that time was exploitive and corrupt. It later became the home of St. Clare and her sisters and had remained a symbol of simplicity and purity for the last eight hundred years.

As she looked upon that same altar, Anna felt something else release inside her, like a knot around her heart being untied, and her heart beginning to relax. She recognized the feeling—forgiveness. She had forgiven her father for pushing her away. And she was forgiving herself for holding onto the bitterness that had nearly poisoned her life. Anna realized she wasn't alone after all. Her mother was with her. And now she had a sister. Profound gratitude flooded her heart.

Anna wished Giovanni was with her to celebrate this final victory. As the sun began to set over the valley she wondered where he was, where he went, and why he had disappeared so suddenly. She wouldn't have had the courage to continue without him, which meant she would have never discovered she had a sister named Marisa. Would she see him again, or would he remain a marvelous mystery she would never comprehend?

Anna was no longer the lost soul that had started this journey, determined to keep God at a distance. Now here she was, sitting in the chapel St. Francis rebuilt with his own hands. Maybe there was a familial chord that connected her to this man after all. The thought of the Poverello now filled her to overflowing. She would never be the same.

As Anna walked through San Damiano's inner garden, she passed a half-open door that led to what appeared to be an office. Ancient paintings and drawings lined the walls, and Anna noticed an old friar hunched over a desk, paging through a large volume of art. He looked up at her and smiled, his long white beard spilling onto the page. Anna lifted her hand to say hello. The priest closed the book and motioned for her to come inside.

"Welcome to San Damiano," he said as she opened the door and stepped into the room. "You're a pilgrim walking from La Verna?"

"As you can see," Anna said, holding up the walking stick she held in her right hand. "I just arrived in Assisi earlier today."

"Is this your first time?" he asked, standing up and walking over to her.

"I was actually raised in Assisi. Today, when I walked through the gate, it was the first time in forty years."

"Forty years? So you were a young girl when you left."

"I was seventeen," Anna answered. "I moved to the US and never wanted to come back. Now that I'm here, I wonder why it took me so long."

"Welcome to your home," the friar said, leaning over to kiss Anna on the cheek. "This is the spiritual home of so many people, but for you it is much deeper. My name is Padre Leone, by the way."

"I'm Anna," she said, holding out her hand. "How long have you lived here?"

"I've been in the Franciscan order for over sixty years and the last thirty I've been here in Assisi. I sit here in my office every day, studying art and trying to live up to St. Francis's example. These ancient paintings tell us so much about his life and what it means to be poor in Christ."

"You know, a few days ago words like that would have set me off," she said to him. "Why would anyone want to be poor in Christ? Now I think I understand."

"Tell me what that means to you now," the friar asked her.

Anna considered the question, her mind flooded by memories of Giovanni and their journey. Without preaching or trying to get her to change, his simple influence had dismantled her defense. And though she resisted it the entire camino, Anna realized she was forever changed. The figure of St. Francis was no longer something to avoid. He was an example of something she had wanted her entire life—a community, a family—and without her even knowing it, it had been in Assisi all along.

"I suddenly realize how poor I was, Padre . . . not in a physical sense but in the important ways. I was angry for a long time, and it kept me from realizing how blessed I really am. Thanks to a friend I met on the trail who told me he didn't believe in a God, but that he believed in ONLY God."

Leone chuckled to himself. "I like that very much. Only God."

"I think that's how I feel now. I don't believe in a God somewhere above or beyond us, but one that is more intimate than anything we can imagine, closer than our breath. All the worldly things we strive after don't matter when you realize that. I think that's what it means to be poor in Christ."

"And that's why I became a Franciscan so long ago," he said. "I had two older brothers who were successful in the world, but I always knew there was something more. I don't think I would have been happy if I had tried to follow their path. The spirit of St. Francis called to me and it hasn't let me go." Then he touched Anna's arm and motioned for her to follow him. "Come here for a moment, I want to show you something."

He walked to a bookshelf and Anna watched as he lifted an oversized volume and placed it on the desk. Dust reflected off the light as it dropped onto the heavy wooden surface.

"That looks very old," Anna said as she stepped behind the desk and joined him.

"It is . . . around one hundred and fifty years old. It's one of the oldest volumes of this book in Italy, not counting what they have hidden away in the Vatican, of course." He opened the book to the middle, carefully paging through until he found what he was searching for.

"Ah, here it is," he said, moving aside so Anna could see. "This is the oldest image we have of St. Francis, painted by a Benedictine monk approximately eight years before he died—1218, as you can see in the description. This is the only painting we can say with near certainty resembles the Poverello."

The picture revealed a thin man with a somewhat gaunt face, clearly the result of the many penances Francesco endured throughout his life. The cowl of his habit, which was pulled over his head, was pointed strangely and his right hand seemed to be hovering over his heart. Anna noted the rope with its traditional three knots, signifying the three vows every Franciscan takes—poverty, chastity, and obedience. She read that the original fresco, chipped and faded by time, was painted on a wall in the Monastery of St. Benedict in Subiaco.

"As you can see, St. Francis is painted without a halo and without the stigmata," Padre Leone said. "This is how he would have been painted if he was still alive. Every painting after his death shows him as a saint; this one shows him as a man."

As Anna looked at the painting she felt a strange feeling of recognition slowly rise in her mind. She knew this face, but from where? Then it suddenly fell into place. Staring at her from an eight-hundred-year-old fresco was the friend she knew and missed. "Giovanni," Anna said in shock, almost without noticing whether she spoke aloud or not. "He looks just like Giovanni."

"What did you say?" the friar asked.

Anna had to catch her breath. "He looks like a dear friend of mine," she said, still in shock with a touch of bewilderment. "Giovanni is his name. We walked together on the camino. The resemblance is amazing."

"Giovanni you said? That's very strange."

"Why is that strange, Padre?"

"Well, you say that he looks like your friend, and that alone would be very interesting. But the fact that your friend is named Giovanni . . . what a wonderful coincidence."

There was no denying the strong likeness. Giovanni looked exactly like the fresco hanging in the monastery in Subiaco, particularly the soft eyes and beard. Impossible—and yet true.

"What are you saying?" Anna asked.

"I'm saying that Francesco was not St. Francis's name."

She turned to him, the spell suddenly broken. "What do you mean? How could that not be his name?"

"Anyone who knows the story of his life knows this," he said. "When Francesco was born, his father was in France buying cloth for his business. It was the custom to name the child for the baptism, which always took place within a few days. There were no exceptions to this. Since Pietro was away, it fell to Francesco's mother, Lady Pica, to choose. When Pietro returned from France and learned the name his wife had chosen, he was furious. He declared his son would have the name he wanted, not what his wife had chosen. From that day on he was known as Francesco, though that was never the name on his baptism records."

"And his real name?" Anna asked, even though she already knew how the padre would answer.

"Giovanni, of course. Francesco's real name is Giovanni."

It was as if a bright light went off inside her. Of course it was true. St. Francis's name was Giovanni. She looked at the painting and everything made perfect sense. She remembered when Giovanni had told her that his father did not like the name his mother had given him and had chosen something he liked better. She also remembered the birds singing on cue, her foot healing so quickly, and the way he communicated with Bevo. Everything suddenly made sense.

"It was him all along," she said, tears blurring her vision. "Oh, Father, you have given me such a gift today."

She wrapped her arms around the priest who, though surprised, returned her embrace. She could feel that even though he didn't understand what had just happened, he could tell it was of Divine importance.

"I was walking with him the entire journey," she said through her tears.

16

THE RETURN

A few days after she returned to Portland, Anna walked up Burnside, toward Powell's Books with the camino guidebook tucked under her arm. She had written a note on the inside cover, hoping that one day—weeks or even months from now—someone might pick it up and read her words. She didn't try to conceal the book as she walked through Powell's front entrance. She was there to replace it on the shelf where it had fallen off and struck her on the head months earlier.

The idea had come to Anna on the flight back from Rome. The perfect ending to an amazing journey. She walked through the stacks and after a moment or two found the right section and shelf, and slid the book neatly into place.

Standing there looking at the spine, she felt a sense of relief. *On the Road with St. Francis.* She didn't realize the title was meant to be taken literally! The thought made her smile, and images of Giovanni flashed through her mind. She remembered when he'd slid the note under her door, wishing her "buon cammino" when she was still at La Verna, and how good it felt to see him when she reached the Eremo di Cerbaiolo after spraining her wrist. Many other scenes came to her, but most of all she remembered his eyes, how they penetrated her heart and helped her learn the power of love and forgiveness. At first she had wondered what she would do without Giovanni in her life, but she realized he would always be with her. And that, in truth, he always had been, even when she was a child.

"Just one more look," she thought, pulling the book back off the shelf. Whoever read her note might never know the details of her journey with Giovanni, but she hoped it would spark something in them. Perhaps her note might inspire the same passion to walk the Camino of St. Francis. Maybe they would feel inspired and go buy a pair of hiking shoes just as she did, fly to Italy, and make their way by train to La Verna. And maybe, just maybe, they would spot a young Italian man sitting in the refectory with a smile that lit up the whole room, and after a little hesitation, sit down with him and start a conversation. If they were lucky he'd become their camino companion and, by the time they got to Assisi, they would have experienced their own life-altering journey. There was no way Anna could know, but there was a chance. Knowing Giovanni, there was a good chance.

She opened the cover and read:

You may think this note was written for someone else, but it wasn't. I'm writing it to you—whoever's lucky enough to pull this book from the shelf and open its cover. It's not by chance that you're reading it now. I bought this very copy and walked the Camino of St. Francis, and I'll never be the same. Maybe you're feeling a flutter of anticipation deep inside you as you read this. If you are, I encourage you to read a page or two. Take a few moments and imagine how it might feel to walk along the paths and small roads St. Francis walked eight hundred years ago. And if you choose to accept the challenge and walk the 110-mile-long camino, I promise you won't be sorry. And, by the way, if you meet a young man named Giovanni along the way, tell him the author of this note says hello.

She closed the book, placed it back on the shelf, and walked away.

AFTERWORD

A couple of notes about what you just read. All the towns and villages mentioned in the story are real, and the trails themselves have been presented as accurately as possible. The only exception is the section regarding the Alpe della Luna nature reserve. Though the reserve is on the camino path, the story I described is not found in any of the early Franciscan sources. It came from my own vivid imagination, and I apologize to the St. Francis purists who noticed this straightaway. Otherwise, everything you've read is quite accurate.

Angela Seracchioli's *On the Road with St. Francis* was an invaluable resource throughout the entire process of writing this book. If you ever consider walking the camino, find it and keep it close on your journey. I remember when I first met Angela many years ago, not long after she wrote her guidebook. Her passion for the camino was contagious and I asked her to arrange two trips for me. I imagined the story of Anna and Giovanni on that first journey, and it has taken me all these years to write it down.

I'm also profoundly grateful to my friend Emese Janiga who sent me Angela's guidebook when she realized my memory of specific places was seriously flawed. She spent days checking and rechecking to make sure I was as accurate as possible when describing all the villages and trails on the Camino of St. Francis. This story would not have been possible without her help.

Most of all, I want to thank you, the reader. Sharing the camino with you was a great gift. I hope one day you'll have the pleasure of meeting Giovanni on some path somewhere. You may not recognize him right away, but there will come a moment when the tumblers fall into place and you will. In fact, I hope it happens to you over and over.

JOIN A GROUP ON THE CAMINO OF ST. FRANCIS

Writing this book has been one of the greatest pleasures of my life. I could feel myself walking beside Anna and Giovanni, remembering many of the places they visited from my own walks from La Verna to Assisi. If you're inspired by the story of Anna and Giovanni, consider joining me on the abbreviated Camino of St. Francis. We will begin in Laverna and walk about three miles per day through most of the villages mentioned in the book, arriving in Assisi on day 10. We'll then spend around four days touring Assisi. This is the trip of a lifetime, and if you want to stay informed, visit WorldPeacePulse.com to register for our mailing list. We'll send out email notifications (months in advance) when we plan our next camino. I would love to see you on a future trip.

Blessings,
James Twyman